FIRST DATE ABDUCTIONS

JUMPING THE *shark*

MATCHED WITH THE SPACE SHARK

ASH RAVEN

Illustrations by Sophie Zuckerman @dextrose.png

Edited by Kai @DerpyWickedFox

No part of this book was created using AI (Artificial Intelligence)

Contents

To all child free folk out there who want an alien romance without procreation, and to me who loved Captain Gantu just a lil too much as a kid

Within These Pages...

Thank you for picking up the first book in my cosy alien romance series, First Date Abductions. This is an adult romance featuring a giant shark man and his human love. Please read through the warning below to prepare yourself, and know that this is not an exhaustive list.

CONTENT TAGS: Plus size female lead, shark man male lead, blind date, alien abduction, anti mars needs women, ridiculous t-shirts, scienced soulmates, and campy but inaccurate space physics

CONTENT WARNINGS: Alien abduction, blood (period and mating bite), scarring (mating bite), consensual aphrodisiac usage, mentions of anxiety and work related stress, mentions of strict and absent parents, and parental death (natural)

SEX RELATED KINKS: Power exchange dynamic, Daddy Dom, hints of DDlg, bratting (unplanned), dupeen MMC with special features, mating frenzy (heat), aphrodisiac saliva, spit play, double penetration, anal play, fluid play, flavoured cum, spanking, thigh fucking, oral sex, and biting

If you think a warning was missing here, please send me an email at ash@authorashraven.com

The Solarium Union System

DISPLAYING THE UNITED PLANET AND SYSTEMS OF THE SOLAIUM UNION AS KNOWN TO PRESENT DAY

DERIVED FROM THE LATEST AND BEST AUTHORITIES

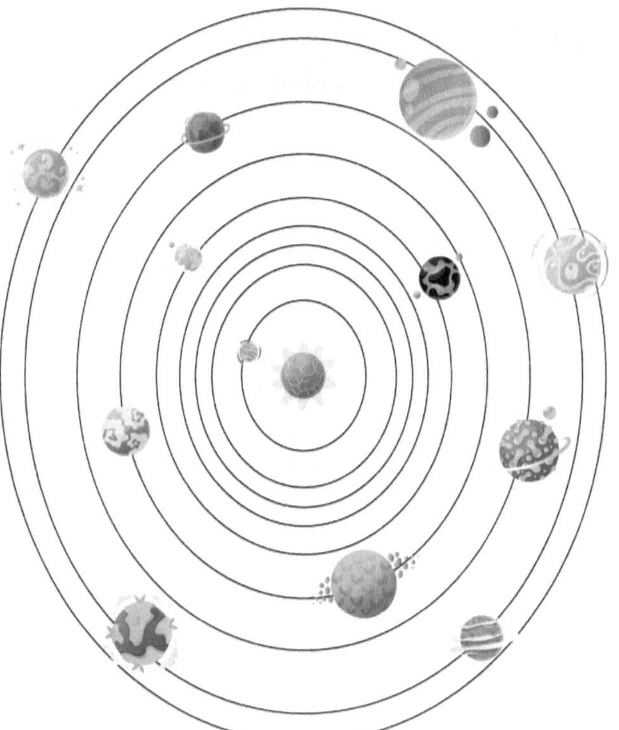

1. AXILARIA 2. BIOTERRIUM 3. ZENITH 4. PALLENIA
5. BRALAVIS 6. NEPHUS 7. HOL'MARIA 8. TOVELARON
9. ERUTA 10. KORTUN 11. OULARA 12. CECARRO

Chapter 1

Ma'xon

Dear Candidate #9247-AX,
Your application for the Terrainne Rehoming Programme has been accepted. Please report to satellite station QVO-97 in two cycles to begin education and training to find your human companion.

·♥·♥·♥·♥·♥·

IT IS A UNIVERSAL known fact that homo sapiens are extremely durable and biologically incapable of breeding outside of their species. They can adapt quickly to nearly any environment they are placed in and come in such great varieties that once they were discovered during a galactic edge scrap, The Solarium Union voted to preserve the planet for science.

Untouched by the other solar systems in our galaxy, there was only a single planet that had inhabitants. They had no concept of indoor plumbing, yet alone the idea that their world was one of many far beyond their own. Even now, in the modern day, these "humans" as they have named themselves, can barely make a manned mission to their only moon. Their satellite technology is so weak that the one that made it out of their solar system takes days to transmit the falsified information the SU has been feeding it. This whole system has been deemed as a special nature reserve so solarium scientists and thinkers can monitor their evolution.

They are a unique and valuable commodity in the SU. It keeps planetary leaders in line when it comes to paying the large tax, knowing they could be hurting their future mate if the planet isn't protected. Some planets suffer from hyper fertility and so much over population that governments will pay to get their citizens to join the Terrainne Rehoming Program. Other planets offer it as a lottery, so each citizen has an equal opportunity to attend the program.

And some planets, like Axilaria, just let its citizens do whatever they want.

This programme has been around for a long time. Long enough that even when I announced to the Senate that I planned to join, there were cheers for my happiness rather than shouts of despair. My sister's lineage will take the place of leadership once we are gone, as is protocol for when the head of a local colony ends their lineage. Before leaving for the TRP, I had quietly transitioned my powers and plans were drawn up in preparation for the mating frenzy that would awaken in me once I found my mate.

I was fully focused on my education of homo sapiens and how to interact on these "blind" dates we would be set up with. To every knowledgeable member of the union, the Terrainne Rehoming Program looks like any government run mating agency, except there are rigorous questionnaires and interviews, along with the full spectrum of medical exams, that happen before you even step foot into a learning simulation. All of this information is fed through a database that also contains all the information on adult humans seeking partners.

The human side is called a "dating app".

Apparently it is easier to get them to attend the programme when it is designed to look like a game. But the humans don't actually know that a part of their agreement with usage of the app is to allow the TRP full access to everything. From hospital records to preferred erotic materials, they get it all. It's how they match humans to other beings.

And I have been matched with a creature so precious, I am concerned I will go into a frenzy before we even make it off planet. I examine the travel pod on the program's ship, triple checking that all the settings are fixed to prepare my future mate for Axilaria.

We are nearing Earth now, and I am anxious. She must be given the most comfortable and easy journey home. It is not long once we get up to speed, but her body will not be adjusted to space travel. And from the training videos, it seemed many humans did not react well to seeing the vacuum of space from space. With the pod, her decontamination and planetary implants can be completed before we land and submerge on Axilaria.

I scrape my four fingered hand against the grain of my scales. Everything will be perfect sailing. My dual pointed tailfin flicks and grazes across the smooth walls and floor of the ship as I pace about. These nerves are downright out of place for a male of my age. By human standard age, my life is nearing its end. I've lived ninety two earthian years. Axilarians easily live to one hundred and fifty earthian years, with a long portion of it being spent in our youth. We aren't considered fully grown until we are fifty.

But she likes an older male, I remind myself.

While different species have different lifespans, humans have the shortest. The TRP wouldn't be as successful if mates were dying off much sooner than their nonhuman counterparts. For my application, the pod has been programmed to only slightly adjust my date's life span, should everything go well tonight. If it doesn't...

That dark thought brings me back to the file on my data screen. Focus on her now, on bringing her home.

Odette (she/her), 28

I have already voiced my concern about our age difference, but according to the TRP it wasn't too unusual for humans to seek mates with a significant gap. And if some of the long form transmissions we have shared back and forth leading up to this blind date are correct, Odette is perfectly happy with our relative age difference and is quite excited for our date tonight.

A shiver vibrates through my fins with anticipation.

"Landing in approximately three ticks. Prepare for body swap and meeting your mate," the cheery automated voice overhead announces.

I take a deep breath. The body swap is the portion of the night I'm most concerned about. Walking around with no tail or fins to keep me centred? I'm going to make a x'rox of myself the first time I meet my mate.

The human body they have given me is proportioned similar to my own body. It is a large male, his skin a pale brown colour that is a similar shade to my grey skin. The head fur—*hair*— he has is short, nearly all black except for a few streaks of silver. The rest of his body is also covered in fine fur. Similar to the Axilarian, there is a layer of fat protecting his muscles.

Unlike the Axilarian male, however, this form only has one cock. Is this even a size impressive enough to attract mates? Despite weeks worth of simulated mating training, I still don't understand how the receiving humans enjoy fucking males so lacking.

It doesn't matter now, my Odette will never see that body's sex organs nor will she find any better than mine.

One cock. What a joke.

I step under the transmitter and put the helmet on, strapping in my midsection to keep me upright. The machine boots up quickly, a hum vibrating my neurons until I pass out and wake up again in the human form. I look down at my body and shiver. Uncanny is the easiest way to explain this feeling. The new skin I'm wearing is much more sensitive, but my nose is not nearly so. I take a deep sniff and can only get the barest hint of sweet rillin oil I spread across my scales to please my mate.

Either way, I brought a spare balm to apply to this skin to add a level of familiarity to this momentous occasion.

There are human garbs prepared for me by the program. Dark, organic, hard-wearing trousers with multiple pockets and some kind of white chest protection vest to prevent the outer short sleeved shirt from touching my now hairy chest. The instructions prompt with the garments say to partially clasp the shirt and tuck the ends of material into my trousers.

I don't understand the appeal of the "blue collar" costume I've been given, but the file said this would appeal to Odette. It also came with a pair of heavy boots that could sink a being just as easily as it could protect their feet. The look is finished with the prerequisite cactus pencil sticking out of the pocket. An odd signifier, but when Odette told me of this writing utensil she had that had a wooden desert plant glued on top, I claimed to have a similar one.

"Please take your seat as we enter the atmosphere. At our current trajectory you will arrive at your required location on time."

This is it. I'm meeting my mate.

Chapter 2

ODETTE

OH NO.

Oh no no no no.

I'm *so* late. This is the exact opposite of how this day was supposed to go. Being late is like a cherry on top of a shit shake. First I spilled coffee on my nice top and had to swap it for an old t-shirt that the radio station had buried in a closet. Then my stupid co-workers thought it would be the greatest idea ever to pull a prank on me and post it on the station's social media feed.

I'm just a sound producer. Everyone knows my voice for radio ads, but nobody can put a face to me. That's the way I prefer it, honestly. I get flustered and tongue tied the moment a camera is shoved in my face. Now there is a video of me, screaming at the top of my lungs, throwing flyers everywhere, as our sports host dances in a lobster suit next to me.

I'm not sure I've ever felt more embarrassed in my life.

So yeah, here I am, parking in the back lot of the Likton County Brewery thirty minutes late, wearing a shirt from 2013 that says "Lik This" with an arrow pointed down at my crotch.

Mason has probably already left. I'm going to walk through the front door of the brewery and find a fifty-something year old guy sitting at the bar with a cactus pencil stuffed into his shirt. Why would he stick around for thirty minutes for a date with a stranger?

I've been stood up before, I know how a person feels at this stage. Like an absolutely unlovable loser. Or at least that is how I felt the last two times it happened. Both times the guys were from other dating apps, though. The first five minutes were fine. At ten minutes, I sent them messages just checking to see if we were still on for our date, because we can all be forgetful. But as it got later into the evening, I just felt that horrible, gnawing sadness in my gut.

A few glasses of wine made me feel better in the moment, but those experiences were enough to get me to switch to something a bit riskier.

At least, it feels risky to me.

The Real People dating app is a blind dates app, meaning until we meet in person, no pictures are exchanged. Everything is done via a rigorous personality quiz and texting. It's basically anonymous, which did take the edge off answering the more explicit questions, but for weeks since I signed up I've been biting my already short nails to the quick about the lack of pictures. The big "what if" question is always on my mind.

I don't even know what Mason sounds like, which is equally nerve-wracking and joyous. My whole life, the one thing people have ever complimented me on was how pretty my voice sounds. Yet here I am worried that I don't know what my date sounds like as if that matters.

It doesn't. I already know the important things about Mason (he/him), 52.

He's smart with A+ banter. Any time work is a bit slow, I always pull up our chat for a good laugh. He isn't local, which is a plus for me. He is the right kind of outdoorsy, meaning he likes lazing in the sun and drinking or floating around in the water. He recently retired from a high stress job, so he's looking to settle down and spoil his partner. I blushed so hard at that message the first time I read it, the studio manager asked if I was having a hot flash.

But maybe none of that matters now. There are no messages from him in the app. I sit in my car for two minutes, waiting for a reply to my message if he is still here while the sci-fi romance audiobook I downloaded at lunch plays through my speakers. Honestly, I wish I could be abducted like this guy. It would solve a lot of my problems.

Like this one, where I'm waiting to see if my date thinks I stood him up.

It's now or never. The best case scenario is that he is still here, and worst case scenario I get to drown my sorrows in boneless buffalo wings and rosé.

I walk through the glass double doors and am smacked in the face by the smell of yeast and hops exactly thirty three minutes late for a date I have been buzzing about all week. There is already an apology forming in my head. Whether I get to say it in person or over text is a different story.

I show my ID to the guy at the door and walk into the warehouse sized space. It's been redone to have that cool industrial vibe, and not the sterile, stainless steel kind that is hidden behind frosted glass near the back.

It's busy tonight, being a Friday in October, but this is crazy to me. I work my way around the edge of the room trying to find a man with a pencil. The gnawing in my stomach grows the longer I spend on my tiptoes peering over at different men. Truly, I'd given up hope by the time a beefy giant of a man nearly runs me down.

"Ope, sorry, p—" He stops mid apology, the hand he caught me by holding onto my hip. So subtle I almost miss it, his large fingers flex against my soft sides.

There's a cactus pencil tucked firmly into his shirt pocket.

"Mason?" I ask, all the nervous energy of the week stealing my voice until it comes out whisper soft. I can already feel my cheeks flaming and it only gets worse when I remember the shirt I'm wearing under my jacket.

"Odette?"

My eyes zero into him like I am in a Hallmark movie. The man before me is suddenly all I can see and the light around us softens into heart shapes floating around his head. Dressed like one of the guys from the charity 'Blue Collar Men' calendar the radio station did last year, this is the man of my dreams. Thick, padded muscles all wrapped up in sturdy workwear, like he just came from the shop or the farm, sets my loins ablaze. There is something about a person who looks ready to get down and dirty that makes me question all my life choices up to this point.

And he's here to meet me.

"Are you okay?" he asks, placing his other hand on my flushed cheek.

This is way too forward for a first date, a blind date at that, but his voice is so rich with just a touch of gravel, that I am completely hypnotised by him. My mind is frozen, but my body is on fire with an urgent need. I'd let him drag me just about anywhere right now as long as he kept talking to me and holding me with this kind of care. His hands are calloused, but not dry when he brushes a thumb over the round apple of my cheek.

"I-I—oh my god, I'm sorry," I stumble over my apology and shock. "Today has been a nightmare to say the least, and I'm so sorry I was late and you waited for me—"

"I'll stop you right there," he says, still holding on to me and letting me stare up into his unbelievable dark eyes. "I would have waited all night for you, Odette."

It's a red flag, but I think I might be in love anyway. He's so warm and everything about him screams comfort and romance. We've been talking for a month, and after all the more salacious things the personality quiz had me answer, Mason must know exactly what it takes to romance me. Just like I know, from what the app has given me, what he is looking for in that area of his life.

"Well, that's not totally true. At some point. I probably would've checked my phone to see if you cancelled," he clarifies, a soft, panty-melting smile forming on his lips. "I'm really happy you showed up."

For a moment, I'm glued to my spot, staring up at this perfect man and wondering what sort of alternate reality I've woken up in. My heart is racing so fast I think I might actually pass out. It's only when someone bumps into me from behind on the way to their own table, pushing me all the way into Mason's chest that I snap out of it.

But almost immediately snap back into my stupor.

Wow, is he *tall*. With both my hands on his chest, my head tilts back far enough I feel my throat being exposed. When he meets my gaze, his eyes are heady and I swear his pupils dilated. We've only been talking for a month, and this is our first time meeting in person, but when I look at him, it feels like magic and science are melding together to make the perfect man for me.

I'm not sure who does it first. Am I pressing up on my tiptoes or is he leaning down? I don't care once his lips are on mine. He tastes sweet and tart like he's been chewing on sour apple bubble gum. I want to lick that flavour out of his mouth and swallow him whole. My fingers curl into his shirt as he digs his hand into my hip. The one on my cheek slides around to hold my head at the perfect angle for him to devour my mouth.

A wolf whistle reminds me we aren't somewhere private where I can do all the naughty things that threaten to burst out of me. There will be no dick sucking in public. The back parking lot still has potential though as long as this keeps going.

"Maybe we should have something to eat?" I suggest, nose still touching his, my lips bumping against his as I speak.

"As long as I can have you for dessert."

Chapter 3

Odette

THAT LINE IS NEARLY as cheesy as the loaded potato skins we order when a waitress drops off our pints. Mason insisted we get a booth instead of the rickety looking folding benches and I couldn't have agreed more. I hate those things. With the table shoved to the far side, I scooch all the way in and he follows in right behind me. Once his arm is tossed behind my head, he has me completely trapped.

I haven't felt this safe on a date in years, maybe *ever*. Even with his body angled towards me, blocking out the rest of the pub, there is nothing but care radiating off of Mason. I hold my pint in one hand, his in the other. He hasn't stopped touching me, holding me, since we bumped into each other.

This is the greatest date of my life.

Mason takes another sip of his beer, the foam catching on the moustache part of his facial hair. I lick my lips, unwilling to stop staring, losing myself in his dark eyes. His thumb rubs over the back of my hand and I want to kiss him again. With the way we sit, half facing each other, anytime someone walks by, I get a whiff of his aftershave as well. It reminds me of lightning, the smell of a big storm about to break and flood the river.

My head falls against his arms as he tells me about his job.

"It's not that I disliked the co-county clerk. It's that he has no taste in landscape design."

"Uh-huh." I nod along, fighting a smile. "Not that he was just trying to remind you of the ordinance against planting invasive species."

"But the blooms, Odette," he laments, twirling a piece of my hair. "They are the most amazing shade of green. Almost like the green in your eyes."

"So you retired because your nemesis saved your town?" I asked.

"No, I retired because I woke up one day and realised I wanted more than my job. There was never any doubt in my head when I chose to work for my local community. It's rewarding, made me feel good for a long time." He sighs and I take a sip of my beer. The metallic taste tickles my nose and makes my cheeks feel all the warmer in my jacket still. "But coming home to an empty house isn't what I want anymore. Calling it settling down makes me sound fucking old though, doesn't it?"

"Yes, but I get that empty houses can be cold. Since my dad moved into the home in Arizona, it's just me taking care of his old house and all the crap he left behind for me."

"When did he move?" he asks.

"A couple of years ago. Just up and decided that he hated how cold it gets here in winter."

I must look sad because Mason squeezes my hand. I shove a potato skin in my mouth because I'm not really sad my dad moved into a home. He's a grouchy asshat of a father who doesn't call, but guilt is a weird thing. I couldn't keep taking care of him when all he'd do was shout about how much I wasn't like Mom. My parents had me later in life and my mom passed while I was at college. The house hasn't been the same without her.

"If you could be anywhere," Mason starts, "where would you want to be?"

There isn't a single place I could think of being right now other than at the brewery with him. His warmth wraps me up like a comfort blanket I had forgotten I even had. *But*, I reminded myself, this is a first date and he is clearly trying to steer our conversation away from such a heavy topic.

"You know that scene that people always use for like tropical vacations commercials? The beach on one side of your home, and a vast untouched jungle on the other side?" I wait for him to nod. "That's where I wanna be. I don't care how humid it is, I want a small private island where I don't have to think about anything to do with my life."

"That sounds like a dream, where do I sign up?"

We laugh, because who doesn't want that imaginary island? We are all trying to escape something, but the longer Mason and I spend talking, the less concerned I am about where that dream place is and more about making sure he is there with me. What would our island be like if we made it together, rather than escaping to one for a two week getaway?

My heart is racing a million miles in front of my head, but I can't bring myself to catch up and think about how insane this is. In fact, I think my life could use a little more crazy and wild, and a lot less taking the slow lane. I'm almost thirty, I need to live a little and have a feral quarter life crisis. I've got nothing tying me down, no extreme debt or family, so why the fuck not? Why shouldn't I take the plunge and just go all in with Mason?

"Are you sure you aren't too warm?" he asks when our plate is long empty and the diet cola I ordered hours ago is just melting ice.

"Oh, I'm boiling alive," I joke. He gives me a chastising look that tells me he's annoyed that I'm allowing myself to even be uncomfortable. "Look, I'm not joking about today being a nightmare. I spilled coffee all down my nice top and I had to wear whatever extras we had left at the radio station."

"I'm sure I have worn more ridiculous things. I'd rather you be comfortable," he says.

The brewery is much quieter now. The high school football game ended about an hour ago, and since our team lost, most people have gone home rather than having another celebratory round. It's almost serene to be here now. On a TV somewhere they are playing an old Pacers' game and I can just see all the servers crowding around the far booth, rolling cutlery into napkins. Things are winding down for the night.

"I'd be more comfortable if we get out of here," I murmur, my warm cheeks lighting up as I make my next request. "Come home with me?"

Mason looks at me like I've just asked him what it feels like to win the lottery. His lips part for a moment before stretching into a large grin that is almost all teeth, making my tummy flip. Giddy, more than I have ever been in my entire life, is the only way to describe how I feel when he slaps a pile of cash down on to the table. He holds out his hand for me and it feels like I'm finally in control of my life and this is just the beginning of something great.

We don't make it to the back parking lot. As we round the corner of the building, my feet don't even hit the gravel. Mason moves fast and even when he stumbles a bit, he still manages to press me up against the prefab wall of the brewery like I'm a flyer for a carwash fundraiser. My heart is threatening to pound right out my chest and I feel amazing, beautiful even. He looks at me like I'm more than an easy first date. It's like I'm the first rain after a long, long summer. Like his ground has been parched for months, and I'm about to soak his fields.

His eyes darken, or maybe it's the flicker of the bug zapper hanging by the gutter, but I swear it's like watching magic happen. The light explodes for a moment and as it dims his eyes almost glow. Mason's thick thigh presses between mine and his hands slides my arms up until my wrists are clasped above my head. He takes great care in adjusting his hold on me to one hand, rubbing his thumb over my pulse. I bet he can feel it jump under his touch.

"Is this alright, Odette?" he asks, his free hand able to roam the curves and dips of my body. My jacket is still on, it's thick enough that it takes a moment to feel the heat of his palm at my waist.

"Yes." I smile, another surge of giddiness washing over me in a way I can't fully explain. It's playful and freeing, something I can't remember ever feeling. From the age I could speak, it had been music lessons and voice coaching. There wasn't much room for childhood wonder or joy between having my knuckles rapped while trying to learn piano.

I barely know Mason, but I want to be playful and fun with him.

"Can I tell you something?" He leans down until his nose can brush against mine, his thigh creating so much friction between my legs that I gasp. "I know that we were matched for many reasons, but pup…"

His sentence trails off into a groan as he kisses my cheek down to my neck, but that little name plasters itself all over any coherent thought I possess. Adorable, squidgy, soft, and precious; that's what puppies are, that's what Mason thinks I'm like. That's all I want to be.

I know from what I could see of his quiz results that Mason likes what I like. On paper, we are a match in all categories. But having it pressed right between your thighs so you can grind on it like a lust-sick nun getting her first taste of sin is the most validating proof I could ever need that love at first sight is real.

"You are setting my hearts on fire," Mason says before nibbling on my jaw.

My pussy clenches at the feel of his teeth and I can smell that sour apple bubble gum still. It mixes with the smell of his aftershave and I'm desperate for more. I bury my nose in his thick hair and breathe in the scent of him. My mouth waters and my clit pulses with the beat of my heart.

Mason pulls back to catch his breath, but just as quickly dives back down to capture my mouth. His tongue traces my bottom lip before I open my mouth for him. The taste of him, the feel of his tongue slipping along mine has me wondering if *I'm* the parched one, sucking on it any time he tries to pull back. My hands shake in his grasp, trembling with a desire to touch him.

But my chest starts to ache. I still need to breathe despite how much I never want to stop kissing him. We are also very much out in public, even though it's late and dark, there are still people at the brewery who could see us if this show doesn't get a move on.

When we part ways he is just as breathless as I am. The hand that had been massaging my waist, keeping me slowly rocking on his thigh, moves to cup my face.

"Can I?" The question half comes out between heavy pants. He has no clue what I'm asking and neither do I really. Can I what? Suck his cock right here? Get his phone number instead of messaging through the app? Make a rain check on boning?

"Use your words," he murmurs, forehead resting against mine. "Ask me nice."

I swallow all the apprehension I can and focus on how good he makes me feel before I ask, "For right now, can I call you Daddy?"

There is a pause and I think may have well and truly fucked this up. Perfect on paper, but not in real life because I'm the idiot who is rushing to the chequered flag, despite the line of failed dates in my rearview mirror. All the blood in my body is threatening to burst from my cheeks as my embarrassment rises.

"Seas above, yes," he groans, a laugh caught in his throat. "Call me that anytime you want, whenever, wherever, Odette. Sounds so right on your pretty lips."

Mason pulls back and looks down at me again. His big body is radiating so much heat, I'm melting into the wall behind me and the man in front of me. He smiles and a giggle comes out of me that I can't control. This is otherworldly perfection. A complete one eighty from my horrible day.

His hand flexes around my wrists and I shiver at the pressure. So big, so strong.

"So you wanna come to my house or not, Daddy?"

"One more kiss, pup," he whispers, tilting my face right just for him.

His lips are closed when they meet mine, soft and sealed tight like he doesn't want me to suck on his tongue again. But then he's flexing his thigh between my legs and it sends jolts of pleasure right through me. I want more of him, I want to drown in the heady sensual comfort he offers me.

He kisses down my neck again, his mouth still firmly closed. His hand moves my shirt and jacket to the side, exposing my shoulder to the cool autumn air. It's nice, but something is clearly going on. I squirm a little, pulling one of my wrists down to touch his neck. If he's going to put his mouth on me I want him to do it. Not whatever this weird middle school kissing is.

"Mason," I whine, trying to urge him to go further or stop so we can take this back to my place. He inhales sharply as my fingers dig into his neck. "Ma—"

The word stutters out of me when his teeth sink into my shoulder. My pussy pulses and my clit throbs as I come so hard everything goes dark.

Chapter 4

Ma'xon

Sweet Sur'lax.

That fucking worked. I hadn't actually believed the capsule tooth they installed into this human suit would work, but it did. My mouth flooded with the Axilarian bonding saliva just like it would when pheromones rise between two mates.

While humans don't have any use of the pheromones they produce, there are visual signs I made sure to be cautiously aware of. Maintained eye contact, lingering touches, even licking one's lips can all be signals of interest in mating. The TRP was careful to instruct us on what these mean in humans and explain that clear, verbal consent—an *'enthusiastic yes'*—is the most important part when engaging humans in sexual congress.

And Odette.

My hearts nearly burst from my gills. Or at least they would have if I had been in my body the whole time. This body's single blood pumping organ was filled with erratic energy the whole night. It also became impressively damp and sweaty, but thankfully my mate didn't notice or care.

Even after my first blunder, almost knocking her right over and then seizing her mouth without that clear yes, she wanted to begin the "date". It will take me a lifetime and half to make up for that. My instincts are all messed up from this human suit. After holding her in my small arms for that short moment, I knew she was it. Odette is my mate and I lost control for a brief moment.

That kiss excited her though. She responded with the vigour of a mate in heat.

Odette is a dream, and I hate having to do this part. She's slumped against my front, her arms tucked between us as I carry her to our ship home. There is no part of me that wanted to lie to my mate, so I had to be careful when answering some of her questions. Yes, I do want to go to her house. Not her human house though. It's our house on Axilaria that I want to return to.

There is a small trickle of blood soaking into her jacket. I swallow the lump in my throat. Knowing something will happen doesn't make it easier. In this body, I can't lick the wound until it scars. At home, when the mating frenzy has us both in its grip and I bite her again, I will make sure she knows how much it means to me that she is with me. That we aren't going to stop until she has healed and my cum is leaking from all her holes.

The sex organ in my trousers hardens. I hate this thing. I can't even quicken my steps to hurry us along because this stupid thing has been plastered to my leg all night. Another reason I don't understand why humans find these spongy things attractive.

A disturbed shiver tracks down my spine as I unlock the ship. Currently disguised as a large utility truck, it's easy to slip into the back with Odette in my arms. While the outside is a primitive vehicle, once the airlock is shut, the inner workings of the space worthy craft are revealed. It is swelteringly warm and humid in this ship after spending an amount of time in this body. The hologram dissolves into a series of neutral blue and grey walls that are popular in long haul ships in Axilaria.

There is the pod, which I immediately place Odette in. She doesn't stir, which does something extremely uncomfortable to this body's stomach. To make the transition easier for her, I remove her heavy jacket. She won't really need this anymore, but I empty out all the pockets to make sure all her valuables are accounted for. She didn't have any other personal belongings with her when we ran into one another and I am not going to risk staying on this planet longer than required to search for more of her personal effects.

Once all her things are separated and placed into a different box to decontaminate, I look back at my Odette. Her skin is flushed a shade of pink that reminds me of home, of the delicate blooms that hang from the roof of my house. The writing on her shirt catches my eye, the bold neon font standing out against the dark material.

"They've spelled that wrong," I mutter, but then I follow the arrow down the round curve of her belly and see that it ends just above her navel. Heat rushes through me.

My brain falters. I don't know how long I stand there staring at her shirt, but there isn't a single thought in my head except licking every inch of Odette. When the pod beeps from being left open, only then do I snap back to attention and realise that this body's single penis is still hard. Clearly that thing has a hidden nerve connecting it to human males' brains that we haven't discovered yet because it seems to steer all my actions.

Gently, I brush my knuckles over her round cheek one last time and close the door. Neural mist sprays from the top and bottom of the pod to hold Odette in stasis for the duration of our journey back to Axilaria.

"We'll be home soon," I promise.

Changing back into my body is a relief. My skin feels hardy again and my tail is back where it belongs. The gills at my side ruffle and a shiver tracks through my fins. When I put the human body back into his tube, I put him facing down. I can't look at him anymore and the sooner he's dissolved back into goo, the better. Less a precaution of humans wishing to remain with a facade version of their mate and more the TRP trying to save money, all the human bodies they use are technically an organic gel they reform for each being.

I can smell the sweet rillin oil on my scales again. Odette smelled some of what rubbed off when I switched bodies, but I hope when she calms down after everything she will find it pleasant. The nerves that I felt before she arrived for our date have now trebled.

What if she hates it all?

It will hurt if she demands to return home, my heart will break at my failure. But if she hates Axilaria, or our colony? There will be no point in living. Having dedicated half my adult life to making our home all that it can be, I can't even begin to imagine how I would handle Odette thinking poorly of it.

Axilaria is paradise because of our people. We have spent generations building an ecosystem for our future. Our forebears built a world of peace and education, surely Odette will be able to see the glory in it?

I am thinking too philosophically. There are bigger problems that first must be overcome. Like my real body or that as we break through Earth's atmosphere, her body is being changed to fit the drastically different conditions of my planet. She will look like all the other humans, but that takes some time to adjust.

Thankfully humans have become more accepting of body modification. I can only hope that Odette is open minded about what's being done to her.

There is also the fact she will be enraged about being lied to by the TRP and me. I've heard of many humans refusing to complete mating rituals until they feel their otherworldly counterpart has suitably made up for the slight. I scratch the scales beneath my dorsal fin at just the thought. Like many planets, Axilaria has a strict process for formal apologies. A three phase ritual to ensure whatever slight committed will not be repeated.

As my thoughts begin to spiral further, plans for how I will apologise to Odette start to form right next to how glorious my cum will look leaking from her pussy, the intercom system turns on.

"Please take a seat as we begin to accelerate to hyperspeed, our calculated time of arrival is eighteen earth hours."

After setting the ship to be fully autopiloted, I move to sit across from Odette's pod. There is a soft blue hue from it that reminds me of home, helps slow the beating of my hearts while being pressed subtly into my seat. There is no movement from her as tiny nano arms fix the jagged bite mark I left on her.

Flat human teeth are barbaric things. The sharpness of an Axilarian's teeth make neat, clean cuts. After generations of evolution, rather than our teeth flattening, they changed purpose. During a frenzy when our glands produce copious amounts of saliva to ensure our receiving partner's well prepared to be fucked for several days. The saliva helps heal bites that are an integral and intimate part of the bonding ritual during a mating. It won't sustain their energies, but I have been told the high it gives humans is similar to a botanical herb they smoke.

Overhead, the light flicks to a sleep setting, and the long shadow of my tail stretches even further across the floor. It's been a very long trip and it would be good for me to sleep before I go into a half mad state. This body hasn't smelt Odette, so it doesn't know. I know how delicious she smells in a sense, but once we are on Axilaria and the pod opens again, there is no telling how intense my reaction will be. I'm old enough, I know my body isn't exactly up to shape for a marathon of mating like my younger self had been. My eyes have to be forced closed still when I'm unable to look away from my Odette.

So good. So wet. So mine.

I sleep for most of the journey when I feel it. My nostril slits flair and I feel the drool on my shirt. If I were capable of feeling embarrassed in this state, I would. But I smell her everywhere. Odette's scent has permeated the ship and I'm losing my mind. The muskiness of it, the touch of her perfume that I couldn't quite smell on our date, it's all flooding my brain with a baser instinct to mate.

She's still in stasis. The pod is secure, but when I turn to look at the box I placed her jacket in, the airlock has released. Decontamination completed earlier than scheduled, which I had hoped to avoid. Does this mean she could wake up early?

"CAT, now," I bark, peeling off my ruined top. My skin chafes against the seat I am strapped to but I can't get up yet.

"We are a tick from breaching the surface of Axilaria," the artificial voice announces. "Please remain seated unless absolutely necessary."

"Like fuck," I curse, palm pressing into the bulge of my trousers.

The sooner I can rub my face all over Odette's jacket, the better. If the frenzy sinks its teeth into me too far from home, I will lose it and rip her free from that pod. Usually, with males of my age, one can release some tension and slow down the mindlessness of it with just the scent of their mate.

I scrabble from the back of the ship towards the table behind the cockpit. The moment it's in my hand, Odette's jacket is wrapped around my face like a scarf. I am surrounded by her scent and have to fumble my way back to my seat. Every inhale is setting my hearts on fire with need. There isn't a thought in my head that isn't consumed with her—spoiling, loving, fucking. Until our final days, I want to do everything for my Odette.

Unbuckling my trousers is quite easy when strapped into this chair. I pull my cocks out with one hand, gripping the base of the pale, twitching shafts while I spit into my other. There is enough of the mating saliva threatening to drip from my mouth that by the time I'm done my cock is slippery. My fist slowly pulls at the foreskin of my cocks until my tips are exposed and I can spread more lubrication on them. The mating fluid I produce does nothing special for me, but for Odette?

It will be *heaven*.

Each of my hands wraps around the engorged heads of my cocks and I squeeze to simulate the pulsing grip of my mate's pussy until the frills release. I'm shaking with need as I stare at her. She looks so at peace while my body is on the verge of exploding. I stroke them slowly, breathing in the scent of her. How I will wrap her body around my cocks, watch them stretch her tight pussy until she can fit both inside of her at once. Saliva fills my mouth once more and I can't stop myself from sinking my teeth into her jacket to quell the frenzy.

It doesn't taste of her, but pushes me higher towards my release. I stroke my cocks faster in matching rhythms, playing with the frills on my bottom while I smear more precum onto my top. My tail begins to stiffen the closer I get to coming. There's something depraved about doing this while she sleeps, but I can't take my eyes off her. My fists move faster and faster and all I want is to be truly surrounded by her.

To feel her touch on my real skin and not be afraid, it's all I truly need. I want Odette to see the real me and feel the same passion she felt for that other body. She has to know that I am the same, if not better, with this figure. I trust that she will, and it's that promise that has me milking ropes of fluid from my cock. Just the idea of her touching me with love and desire is all it takes to send me hurtling into the mindless bliss of my orgasm.

Cum covers the space between my spread thighs and finally the haze begins to recede. I swallow any remaining saliva as I stroke my cocks until they are soft. Each sensitive length is carefully placed into my trousers, and the ship's small robot cleaner shoots out from its nook by the pod and all evidence of my act is mopped up by the machine. Overhead the lights slowly rise until they are nearly blinding.

"Prepare to breach the surface of Axilaria."

"Shit," I mutter, sitting up straighter.

I need to make myself presentable so I can truly meet my mate.

Chapter 5

ODETTE

TYPICALLY, I DON'T MAKE a habit of passing out after a partner makes me come. But then again, I've never had a more life changing orgasm that literally made me black out the moment it hits me. It was like my body sang with pleasure for the first time. The stars and planets aligned as Mason hit high note after high note until my mind and body shattered into the best fuck of my life.

I'm going to have to chain him to my bed to keep him around. After that, I can't give this man up. Even after my lateness, he was nothing but sweet and so passionate. He had the kind of magnetism that you only see in movies that kept drawing me closer and closer. I'm certain if he could have pulled me onto his lap, he would have. I wanted his touch on every part of me.

That app is getting a five star rating from me and a fucking glowing review.

Whatever planet they found Mason on, they've struck gold.

"Pup," he whispers and I scrunch up my nose as I'm not exactly ready to be alive again. "Odette, it's time to wake up."

Mason touches my shoulder, but I refuse to open my eyes. Reciprocation is on the menu tonight, but I need a couple more seconds to wrap my head around coming so hard I pass out. As if I'm going to let the night end without sucking his dick. The man waited thirty minutes for me and then did all that? He should be given a whole sheet of gold star stickers.

I'm struck with the need to sneeze and pee all at the same time. I move to pinch my nose and something hard stops my fingers. My body jerks hard as I'm overcome with it. A shiver tracks down my arms and I touch my nose again to make sure I'm not smearing boogers everywhere. There is something metal and looped through the septum of my nose.

My eyes shoot open.

I am not in my bedroom. Or a dark basement, which I suppose is a win since I don't know where I am. It's sunny and deliciously warm and I'm lounging on some kind of fainting couch. There are red and pink bell flowers hanging from blueish grey plastic beams on the ceiling. Is this some kind of luxury hospital?

Beyond feeling like my bladder is going to burst, I feel the best I have in years.

Crouched next to me is a giant grey shark man. That is the only way to describe it. I freeze, slowly moving my eyes down the broad shoulders to exposed arms. There are fins on his forearms and the hand on my shoulder only has four, thick fingers. I flick my gaze back to his face. His eyes are a dark, sparkling grey colour, and there are slits where his nose would fit. They flare the longer I look at him and I'm concerned prolonged eye contact is bad so I look down at his feet.

They are big, and bare, with five toes. I guess I should be happy he has regular feet, but his toenails are as sharp as his teeth. But then my eyes catch on something slowly moving back forth behind him. A tail, like a massive shark's tail with pointy tips and all.

Oh my god.

"Bless you," it says with Mason's voice. "The oxygenator can take a couple of minutes to adjust to."

"Ma—" My voice cuts as I look at the sharp, white teeth in his mouth. "Mason?"

"Ma'xon is how I usually pronounce it," he says, the grey of his skin turning navy. Like he is blushing at telling me how to pronounce his name. "I know this is a lot."

I nod hurriedly as a cramp settles between my legs.

"But you are completely safe here."

"Not if I pee my pants," I say, my voice coming out tight like that will keep it from happening.

His eyes go wide, and suddenly I'm flying. Ma'xon picks me up like I'm a small doll and carries me out of that room into some kind of massive bathroom. He sets me down right by a new age, backless toilet and my knees nearly give out like I haven't used them in a long time. A pack of wipes is set on the sink next to it. Then he is gone without another word, closing the door firmly behind him.

"It locks automatically," he shouts through the door.

That's all I need to know before I'm ripping my pants down. It doesn't occur to me that he might be filming this, but honestly I don't care. This is happening right now. When I am done, I pick up the wipes and read the label.

Biodegradable hygiene wipes for sensitive skin. Perfect for pups, humans, and other soft lifeforms

I'm not sure how I should feel about him having these at the ready. Seeing as there is a locked door between us now, asking him seems the most sensible course of action. For my own sake, I finish up first.

After using the step stool that I didn't see at first to get off the toilet, I step on a small platform to look in the absurdly large mirror over the sink. It's clear everything has been modified to accommodate someone much smaller than him.

Does he have a lot of short, soft guests? Or is this for me?

As I wash my hands, I take in all the parts of me. My hair could probably use a wash, blonde strands extra flat from the sheen of sweat stuck to my forehead and I'm still wearing this god awful shirt. Beyond the small septum piercing there is nothing obviously wrong with me. My body is the same as it was when I got dressed for my blind date.

When my hands are dry, I touch the thing on my nose. It's a simple silver loop. Nothing happens as I make faces in the mirror. Ma'xon called it an oxygenator, so I guess that's like a breathing device.

Are there other devices in my body that I don't know about?

"Hey," I call out, ignoring the button by the door that is currently light. "Why did you pierce my nose? Also why do you speak English?"

"The air on Axilaria is dense and humid, it helps off-worlders adjust and breathe," he answers quickly enough that it makes me think he stood by the door the whole time. "And also during transport, there was a small implant placed in the Broca and auditory area of your brain to help with speech and translations."

I shove my finger up my nose. What good it will do I don't know, but I have a vague idea that my nose connects to my brain. My nostrils are fine.

"Is Axilaria code for something or like..." I trail off. This can't be what I think it is, because then my dreams would be real and that means all those romance novels weren't lying.

"It's a planet, about two systems away from Earth's. It is a part of an intergalactic union of planets. Your planet is a sort of, uh..."

"What?"

"Nature reserve?" he says it like a question. "When it was discovered aeons ago that your planet contained sentient life, it was decided by the Solarium Union to preserve it."

"So I'm like a zoo animal to you?" I demand. "And you abducted me to be some human pet?" Oh no this is *not* my dream. Being a science pet is not sexy.

"Fuck no." He sounds upset, but then there's a thump and groan. "It's a little complicated, and I promise we can have a full history lesson on this, but that dating app you used is a regulated programme designed to help beings find mates in humans."

That statement is more loaded than the potato skins we ate at the brewery, but my mind snags on one word. Mates.

"Like werewolves find mates?"

"I don't know what a werewolf is, Odette." He laughs, and it sounds just like it did on our date; all warm and comforting. "The TRP has matchmaking down to an atomic science. When you sign up, you agreed to them doing a total sweep of you. The personality quiz is just the surface of it."

"Damn," I murmur. "So did you get, like, all my blood work? Do you know my life story?"

"Sur'lax, no," he says. "That's a breach of privacy. All data is secured on a satellite station run by some anally retentive android. We received the same information, the only extras I got were a full cycle of schooling and your picture once we matched."

I slap my palms together in front of my face like I'm praying and press my fingers to my lips. This is fucking insane, and I'm not freaking out. Why aren't I panicking? Is it because I'm not surprised aliens exist? Is it because I was literally wishing I could be abducted by aliens and now it's happened?

Earth is a nightmare of capitalism and war and bad smells. Who would want to invade a planet like that? It makes sense with all our chaos we'd be observed for science. If anything, Ma'xon has saved me from that hellscape.

"Do I have to get a job?" I voice my question out loud.

"If you want, but I figured we'd spend at least twenty five years just being with each other."

My brain stalls. "How old are you?"

"Ninety-two in Earth years, but—"

I push the button that opens the door to the bathroom. "You are not."

Ma'xon is to my left, forehead firmly planted on the wall. There is a massive fin that forms at the back of his head. The base of it connects at the top of his shoulder and the tip ends a few inches lower. He peers over at me, but doesn't hold my gaze.

"I will live for another sixty years approximately, just like you will," he huffs. "You were also given a small injection that slows your ageing to match mine. If I were younger, it would be even slower."

My mouth pops open. That's over a hundred years. He—his people, live that long? I'm not sure what I would do if I lived that long. Ma'xon slowly turns to look at me, his gargantuan body towering over me. He must be eight feet tall. My neck cranes all the way back to look into his eyes.

Is he waiting for me to make a run for it? Obviously, he didn't look thoroughly enough at my personality quiz. There is not a part of me that has that fear instinct. I'm a deer in the headlights kind of gal. But more importantly, I'm not scared of him.

"Did you lie about anything else?" I ask, thinking that will help clear any more of the air between us. When I cross my arms over my chest, my skin is slick with sweat. Damn, it really is humid. Should I be concerned about dehydration?

He pauses, big hand scratching the base of his fin. "Well, I'm technically the former leader of this colony, not just a random employee for the government."

"Monarch or elected leader?" I ask, squinting at him.

"Monarch, but my role was like that of a mayor on Earth. We have an elected senatorial body that rules for the planet. Also our familial line can be removed from office with a simple vote by the colony."

"I'm too dehydrated for that to make complete sense," I say, waving away any concern I had about rulers or freedom.

"Does it need to make complete sense right now?" he asks, while nodding down the hall.

Ma'xon doesn't scoop me up off the floor this time, instead placing a large hand on the small of my back to guide me to a kitchen area. It's warm and I'm reminded of how he couldn't take his hands off me on our date. Is he scared to touch me now?

This place is like the loft apartments I used to dream about when I thought I would move to New York City. The walls are cool neutral tones and colourful potted plants fill any area where the sunlight hits. Like the bathroom, everything has been modified with an additional step for me to come up to a reasonable height.

It's all very domestic and I'm just a smidge tiny for it. But it also means when I heave myself up onto the stool at the bar I don't feel too big. There is an odd comfort in feeling this small for once. I watch him pull out a jug of water from a hidden fridge cabinet and pour the glass in front of me.

"It's filtered, since our water has a slightly different molecular structure," he explains.

"Don't drink the spicy water, got it," I say.

The glass is so big I have to hold it with both hands. But it tastes like water to me.

Wow, being abducted by an alien is really not the scary horror show that movies make it out to be. I don't even have that awkward feeling of being at a friend's house for the first time. There's the urge to snoop through all his things, but I don't feel like I should be concerned if my shoes are on or off. There isn't a sense that he wants me out of his space either. If anything, Ma'xon wants me here and he's done an immense amount of renovating to make it suitable for both of us to live here.

I look around at everything again and just feel at home. Except there aren't blankets everywhere like there are at my house. Then again, I wish I had my bathing suit and some shades with the weather this nice. My gaze drifts to the open doors, a sheer long curtain blowing in the breeze. There isn't a thought in my head about running away. My only concern is whether or not Ma'xon has a pool or if there is a public one we can take a dip in.

From the corner of my eye, he shifts his hand down under the counter. I have a mind to ask him what he thinks he's doing, and he opens his mouth.

"There is—"

"Mai'mai?" someone shouts very loudly outside. "You two decent?"

The navy colour is back in his cheeks instantly. While I don't think my shirt is decent for anyone on Earth, it's going to have to do for Axilaria. I watch his four finger hand scrub down his face before he walks around the counter. Along the way, he brushes his hand across my thigh and for a moment I feel that same heat from the brewery. My fingers twitch to grab onto him, but he's already out the curtain door.

"What possibly can't wait for a few days?" he shouts.

"Your nieces," they shout back and suddenly there is a thundering of feet up stairs.

It only takes a few moments before there is a loud guffaw from outside the door and secret whispers. From here, I can see the outline of two tinier versions of Ma'xon outside. Should I go outside too? I'm sure I'm allowed, but this seems like a family reunion and I don't want to spoil it for them. Giggles erupt and then there's the sound of more feet on the stairs.

"You've been home for hours and you don't even bother to send me a message. You don't even smell like a frenzy. Sur'lax."

The stranger sounds like my type of person. I can't stop the smile on my face when a relatively small, grey head peers through the curtain. I wave before jumping down off the stool. The girls gasp and come rushing in, slamming into me like they had with Ma'xon.

Except, I'm not an eight foot tall beast of a man. We topple over like dominos into a pile arms and tails and more giggles. The three of us are about the same height, but the extra fins makes it hard to find my footing.

"Ke'lee, A'la, you weren't raised in a Zoller," a woman snaps, but there is no bite in her words. She sticks out her hand to help me up once they roll away and says, "I'm Pri'za, Ma'xon's younger sister. The one with the pierced fin is Ke'lee and toothless is A'la."

"Odette," I tell her my name. "What's a Zoller?"

"I think your equivalent is a bae-urn?"

"Barn," Ma'xon corrects her pronunciation, while Pri'za mimics a chatty motion with her fingers.

Like her brother, she is ungodly tall. While slightly leaner, she still looks like she could take down any professional linebacker with a light shove. Her tail sways back and forth behind her and I try not to take offence when her nostrils flare at me. I'm sure I smell a little funky and the humidity is really making me sweat. Any deodorant I had on is long gone by now.

"You don't smell like him." She turns back to look at Ma'xon. "Do you need to see the practitioner?"

"Mai'mai has space cooties," Ke'lee says with a sing-song voice, the jewels on her piercing tinkling as she shakes her head.

"And I'll give them to you two if you don't go play outside," he growls and chomps his sharp teeth at the girls until they are giggling again and running out the door.

"Those aren't a real thing," Pri'za assures me with a smiles. "And we aren't staying, I'm sure the frenzy will get you both soon and nobody wants the sloppy details. We confirmed you're both alive, so I can actually get back to work."

She points at Ma'xon and then waves, gone as quickly as she came with her daughters. He waits a few moments and then falls onto the couch. I stare at him, taking a moment to gather the feelings I have about the whirlwind meet and greet with his family. They seem nice, brash and caring in a way I'm not used to. There is clearly a much closer bond between them than I ever got close to having with my parents.

Will I get to be a part of that closeness?

A scrape noise catches my attention and Ma'xon's heavy tail flexes around the couch as he adjusts himself into a better position. His thick thighs spread wide and I catch a glimpse of the large bulge in his tight pants.

I peel my eyes away from it and land on his broad torso. It's only now that I notice the panelling on his tank top. The sides aren't stripped, they are sheer and something around the upper part of his torso flutters as he heaves another breath.

Gills. He has gills.

He really is like a shark man. Which brings me back to the word his sister used. *Twice*. What the heck is a frenzy on this planet? 'Cause I have certainly watched my fair share of shark week, but I don't think that's what she was talking about.

"I'm sorry about the splash by," he says. "It's not exactly polite, given our situation, but I haven't seen them in a while because of the training program."

"The frenzy thing?" I guess that's what he means by situation.

"It's what I wanted to talk about," he swallows, "before they descended on us. Can you come sit with me, pup?"

Ma'xon pats the spot on the couch next to him, but I'm still thinking about how much we couldn't take our hands off one another on our date. He's being very cautious now, beyond taking me to the bathroom he has done the absolute most to keep his hands to himself.

I take a deep breath and dive head first into the new sea I've found myself in. He looks at me intently as I walk up to him, swallowing noticeable as I stand between his legs. This is where I've wanted to be for hours, I remind myself. There's no reason for worries. I plop down onto one of his spread thighs and pick up his hand to hold in both of mine.

"You can tell me anything, Daddy."

Chapter 6

Ma'xon

Hearing her say that word, syphoning out all the intricate little details of her voice that I couldn't hear in that human suit? I can't open my mouth for fear I'm going to bite her instead of explaining the mating frenzy. My mouth won't stop watering and even before Pri'za arrived I struggled to hold myself back.

Seeing Odette unafraid of me to start and then smiling at my family was like being lost in the seas above and falling onto the softest beach. Any apprehension I had about her adjusting to life here is floating away. She slips into it all like water between my fingers.

Now the only thing that needs work is us. And my hopes are rising at that the longer her little hands hold my massive fingers. I swallow again, trying to keep my mating saliva to myself as I think about our size differences.

"The frenzy is a *mating* cycle," I start, my face heating like a younger male attempting to snare his first love.

"So really like werewolves." She nods and her cheeks turn a lovely red shade.

"What is a werewolf?"

"Oh, they're a classic shifter monster," she says excitedly. "They usually are people bitten by another werewolf, and on the full moon they transform into half-wolf people, and sometimes if the book is really good the werewolf love interest goes into this uncontrollable heat and they have to fuck it out of their system. Too much hair for me, but I get the appeal."

"And what is the appeal?" I ask, unable to keep the amusement from my voice. Already I love her voice. The way her lips form the words and her finger flex around mine when she says uncontrollable heat has my hearts racing.

"It's the undeniable need, the big scary monster overpowering its mate, and the fluids."

"This wasn't part of your quiz." I grin.

My free hand moves to support her, rubbing up and down her damp back. Even as my brain wants to shut off any other thought outside of claiming Odette, there is also the more selfish need to provide for her. Even to simply get her another glass of water, to build her a dry sauna in the back of the house, even to parade her around as my precious mate in everything I can possibly buy her—I want to give her everything I have.

"I mean, I told it I liked romance novels and after everything I had to admit on that quiz I was going to keep something to myself." She huffs a little before her pout softens into a smile. "Is that what your frenzy is like?"

"Surprisingly yes," I say, relaxing a little more on the couch. "It can last anywhere from a day to five days. Usually the purpose of them is to breed, but humans are unique in that they can't reproduce outside of their own kind."

I pause and wait to see how Odette will react to that. Her eyebrows rose when I said five days, but as her shoulders relax and her hands start to wander up my forearm, I don't believe she really cares about having kids. Another note of apprehension to float out of my subconscious. This is going surprisingly well.

"Axilarian's generally mate for life," I continue. "Our saliva produces an aphrodisiac that helps ease the intensity and friction of the cycle. The bite is a clean and—"

"Oh my god," she gasps. "That's how you made me cum? Do you only do that once?"

She stares at me with an intensity I struggle to read, but I won't lie to her. Her quiz results were clear about what she enjoyed sexually, but practice is different from theory.

"It's common for many adult Axilarian's to have multiple bites in one frenzy cycle, but I understand if that doesn't appeal to you."

"Oh no, I want to at least try, the first one hurt like a bitch but the payoff was so worth it."

We both begin to laugh at her blunt assuredness and I can't believe how comfortable this all is, how easily she has accepted all this. There were long sessions during my training cycle about managing distraught humans and what to do to help them adjust to all new information they receive. Odette just is. She exists and is therefore content. She wiggles a bit on my lap until she is close enough to relax on my shoulder.

"Alright, what else?" she asks. "Keep me fed and hydrated and this frenzy thing will be easy as pie."

"Well it will take a bit of work." I clear my throat. I'm not sure how I have made it this far without preparing for this conversation. How does one tell their mate they have not one cock, but two, and that compared to what they may be used to, they are both much larger. They may be incredibly durable, but humans are also cautious when it comes to their reproductive organs.

"The stretching," she murmurs, nodding as if a simple exercise routine for her vaginal muscles will solve any issues.

"There is no polite way to say this, so to be blunt, I have two cocks and they aren't humanlike, Odette."

She freezes on my thigh. Her lush backside tenses so much her body rises slightly. When I inhale again, her arousal washes over me. My cocks thicken and she must've felt them, how can she not? Odette looks at me and before I can stop her, slides onto her knees between my spread thighs. Her hands rest on my legs gently and I must be drooling. Perhaps I won't live another sixty years, I will drown here in my mating saliva as I watch my human.

"Can I see them, Daddy?" Her voice is whisper soft now and my hearts nearly skip a beat.

That little human kink will be the death of me. Her dulcet tones say the word and I am ready to tear apart the system for her. She slips her hands higher up my inner thigh and a shiver races through my fins. The small shake wakes up my senses enough to remember my education.

"Do you consent to the mating frenzy, Odette? I won't hurt you, but it's a very intense and intimate commitment."

"Yes, Ma'xon," she says. "Do you consent to being my Daddy Dom?"

"I meant when I said I want to spoil you, pup, calling me your Daddy just sealed your fate to the seas above."

She sighs with such relief, her joy is almost palpable. The way her shoulders ease, the way her lips curve into a smile, that tells me she is giddy for whatever this first time will bring for us. My hand cups her cheek and she nuzzles into my palm with such pleasure my gills stutter.

It's getting hard to focus. My vision tunnels in on Odette, all the minute details from the spattering of dots on her cheek to the way her nipples press through her shirt now despite the heat. I want to see them, suck on them like I have learned humans like, and most of all I want to leave teeth marks around each of her breasts. My mark will decorate all the parts of her body she will let me.

Her fingers brush over my cocks and my hips jut forward. Even through the durable bioprene material of these pants, the slightest touch is nearly my undoing. She palms them for a moment, teasing me with the heat of her hands. Odette is keen though. Perhaps she realises that I am missing some of those more human attributes, but her fingers fumble over the clasps of my trousers for a second before she pouts up at me.

"Watch me," I command, pressing the release button and then pulling the cords apart to open them.

"Space pants," she grumbles, rising up on her knees. "Can I have a kiss please?"

I stare at her, aching to say yes. There should be no reason to deny her, but I want her to see all of me before she experiences what my saliva can do to the mind. Instead of answering, I rip my shirt off, miraculously not getting caught on my fin. She looks up at me with anticipation, wetting her lips as she stares at my torso.

"Should those be a no touch zone?" she asks, fingers dancing over my soft middle but staying away from my gills.

"They are very good for teasing, but I think you've done enough of that, pup."

The grin on her face is like the sun over the sea. It lights up my world and warms my soul. Her hands digging into the front of my trousers set my scales on fire however and already my frills are emerging from their heads, ready to spray cum everywhere. She pulls them out one at a time. Her soft lips part and I am certain I will be the first male to drown in his own mating saliva in Axilarian history. Odette's cheeks are stained red and I love the colour on her.

Slowly she strokes foreskin back on both of them and the purple frills release and wiggle with their newfound freedom. I know that the human jaw can't naturally unhinge, but she gives it an honest try. Her dimpled chin meets her chest and silence descends between us.

I swallow everything in my mouth, hopefully my tongue as well because I'm staring at the empty space between her fingers. Sweet Sur'lax. She is so small and it makes my thoughts swim with filth I didn't even know I was capable of. She licks her lips again, gulping when she is finally able to close her mouth again.

"There is no rush, and we can—"

She swallows the head of my top cock. Her mouth stretches wide open and my eyes cross. Her moan is one of surprise and suddenly she is stroking her left hand with an earnestness until light purple fluid wells at the frills. She sucks and pumps my cocks as if she has been the one to attend a cycle of training on how to please her mate. Tingles shoot through my tail tips and my body shakes with a need to take over. But watching her work my cocks is almost addictive.

When she pops off one cock, spit dribbles from her lips and she heaves for air.

"Oh my god," she says.

I don't get another word in before she descends on my bottom cock. Now there is so much precum around the head it drips onto the couch. I don't even care. Her lips seal around the tip and she sucks.

Her moans echo around my home and it's sweet music. What will it sound like when it is no longer muffled? Will she sing with ecstasy once she takes my cock? Odette's tongue sweeps between the soft frills and I grit my teeth to stop from spilling too soon.

"Fuck," I groan. I can't keep my mouth shut, I can't care if there is drool on my chest. My mouth opens and words flood from it. "Fuck, I can't get over you, pup. How you're so good for me, it's too much. I'm gonna make an absolute mess of you."

She pops off my cock, her lips swollen. "What if I like it messy, Daddy?"

I grab her under her arms and she giggles when I haul her up to me again. Her plush thighs spread wide over my lap and cocks are now trapped, leaking underneath her gorgeous backside.

"I'm gonna kiss you now. It's gonna feel good, I promise, pup, but it's gonna make everything sensitive and needy." My hands rub up and down her sides, fingers digging into the rolls of her body and squeezing all her softness.

"As long as you're taking care of me, Ma'xon," she whispers. "That's all I want."

My hearts thud against my gills and the frenzy takes over me. Her mouth is smaller than mine, but as it opens for me she still does that little sucking thing she did to that other body. Her lips seal around my tongue and she moans with utter pleasure. Her tongue plunges into my mouth without fear, chasing more of the mating saliva and I have a split second to watch my teeth.

Her body sinks slowly, her movement less urgent and more luxuriating, until finally she breaks the kiss to breathe.

"Wow," Odette says, eyes slow to focus on me again.

"I will always take care of you," I promise, standing up and holding her to my torso. Again she giggles and I want to spend the rest of my life hearing that sound. "Daddy's got his pup."

Chapter 7

Odette

SOMEBODY CALL LIFE ALERT, I have fallen and can't get up. I'm never leaving. Ma'xon is never leaving. We're going to become some kind of bedridden sex maniacs. He hasn't even fully taken his pants off and I'm still wearing my shoes, but Mary mother of *god*.

The giant shark man tastes like salted caramel. No word of a lie, it's like his body is producing my most favourite fall treats. Between his arousal and his mating fluid stuff, I could never eat again and be happy. It's sweet and tart and salty and everything a girl could want. Pineapple has nothing on this.

I'm giddy and giggling uncontrollably as he carries me like a baby out of his front room and into a bedroom. My focus isn't on the décor, it's solely on kissing every part of him I can latch onto. The texture of his skin is a little rough on my lips, but it just makes me giggle more. When he plops me onto what I think is a waterbed with how it ripples under my weight, it's more of the same. I can't stop the sounds from coming out of me.

He was not joking about that aphrodisiac. Will he spit it in my mouth? What will it feel like when he eats my pussy?

"How are you feeling, pup?" he asks, slowly taking off my shoes. He hasn't stopped rubbing me, feeling all my pudgy bits that I have told past partners not to touch. But there is something about the way he looks at me. Sure it's hot and heavy, but there is wonder to it. Like Ma'xon is just as surprised by our coupling as I could be.

"Feeling good," I hum, eyes turning a bit heavy. "Is this gonna make me sleep?"

"No, and I won't mate you if you aren't awake," he explains gently. "I'm going to take off your clothes. Can you sit up for me?"

This is definitely a waterbed. It takes a steady four fingered hand to help me into an upright position. Ma'xon hasn't said a word about my shirt. After spending so long being self conscious about it, I'm offended that he hasn't made a joke.

"Do you like my shirt?" I pout. "I hate it, but it's all that fit."

"It certainly gave me ideas," he says, grey eyes big and sparkly. "Arms up."

My arms fly out on command and he finally laughs a little. When his knuckles graze over my bare skin, all the humour leaves the room. I gasp as goosebumps erupt across my whole body. My skin heats under the delicate touch as he peels my damp shirt from my body. When his hand slides across my belly to my pants it's like his fingers are directly connected to my clit.

"Ma'xon," I whimper.

"I know, I know, pup, it's a lot," he hushes me, but then he rips my pants right down the middle.

The fabric tears, digs into my hips, and when the warm air hits my skin I want to cry with relief and lust. In the few minutes since we've been in here, since I could feel the effects of the mating frenzy, my body felt like it was expanding. Losing my tight pants is like ten pounds of sugar finally busting out of that five pound sack. My body is free to relax and jiggle and exist out of those tummy tuck jeans.

My hands slap onto his bulging biceps. The smack echoes and I giggle, but he flexes under my fingers more. His big muscles are so strong and all mine now. My hips jut forward, and an unholy need for friction, for more, becomes my sole focus.

"Oh my god," I gasp. "Five days?"

Am I going to be like this for five days? This...this needy and sensitive? I'm seconds from cumming untouched and still hungry for cock. This might kill me, but at least I will die the happiest woman alive.

"Do you think you can take it?"

He isn't asking out of fear, he's asking to tease me. I can tell by the curve of his mouth, the slickness on his lips. He's stripped me down and he's shucking off his pants. When we are both buck naked, I've reached a new level of horniness. Five days doesn't feel like it will be enough to make this ache in my pussy go away. I stare at his flushed features, the way the tendons in his neck flex and how his hard, padded torso stretches. Even his tail slowly moving back and forth behind him has me hypnotised.

"Let's find out," I say, falling back onto the bed and spreading my thighs.

My pussy lips open and the air teases my hot skin all the more. I've never been this wet before. My adult life has been one of heavily lubricated sex, and for a hot second I think I might not need it. But then my appreciative gaze snags on Ma'xon's heavy cocks pointed down at me.

Definitely still a must have.

"I'm gonna prep your little pussy and we're gonna see if you can fit one of my cocks in you." He grins.

"Lube me up, Daddy."

I need to stop giggling. At my own joke, at my situation, it's all hilarious though and completely unreal. Maybe it's the saliva, maybe it's the massive fucking weight taken off my shoulders, but I'm so freaking happy I was abducted by an alien.

The fact that he is hot as sin just makes it all the better. Ma'xon is like a wet dream I never knew I wanted.

Watching him pop one of his beefy fingers in his mouth, I reach down to tease the opening of my pussy. A finger slips in so easily, but my muscles still squeeze. When I pull my finger out, it's slick and shiny.

"Trade with me, pup," he says, voice low and husky now.

As he lowers his finger to my pussy, I raise mine up to his mouth. We moan in unison, practically harmonising on instinct. My pussy grips onto him for dear life, trying to suck up any of that mating saliva it can. Ma'xon's teeth barely scrape against my finger and my skin sings. He licks the juices off my finger slowly before he places it back in my mouth.

The mating saliva lube works magic on me. It's giving me the best high I've ever had, but it's not making me blurry like too much weed does. It makes everything more. I can smell the ozone on his skin and there's a tart and salty caramel apple taste in my mouth. His finger slips in and out of my pussy with so much ease there's a second I feel almost embarrassed.

Then he spits on my clit.

Everything in my soul pulses. My pussy clenches around his finger until I see god and all the angels. My body feels like a church choir, the crescendos of my orgasm echoing off all the dusty rafters that haven't experienced pleasure in years. His thumb swirls around my wet clit, keeps my body singing for him.

Ma'xon hums, "That's it, pup, you're doing so good for me."

He leans over me, an arm on one side as his hips spread my legs wider. His cocks rest on my tummy and when I look down I imagine both of them stuffing me full. The little frills on the head tickle. A gasp more than a giggle comes out of me when Maxon starts to pump his finger again, crooking it up to tease me.

I can't believe he knows this much about human anatomy. This is more prep and foreplay than I have ever gotten from a partner in my entire life. His pacing is tantalising and tormenting, but he is so consistent that I barely feel the second finger slide inside.

He hasn't taken his eyes off me either. The longer Ma'xon stares at me the more I want him—fuck me, bite me, kiss me. I want it all, but I'm already shaking on the edge of another orgasm. My hands grab on his shoulders and my hips press up to meet his thrusts to bring it on faster.

"Daddy, I'm gonna come," I moan.

"Is it because your pussy is greedy for my cock?" he teases, thrusting deeper inside of me, but not quicker.

I nod because I can't get any more coherent sounds out of my mouth. It's moans and hiccupped gasps that are timed with him playing my pussy like he's owned it for years.

The maddening motion of his fingers brings on a different feeling I've not had before. Not exactly the same as when I woke up, but fuck me this is the stuff you read about in trash women's magazines or sexual health rabbit holes.

I'm going to fucking squirt.

I hope at least, but either way today, this week, is going to be an eye opening and no holds back experience for the both of us. I'm going to ride this wave until we are both exhausted and satisfied.

There is a gushing sound as my lower half rises a final time to meet him. Little droplets falling onto the floor and even more splattering across my thighs because he hasn't stopped pumping inside of me. My pussy clenches hard and waves of post nut delirium wash over my body.

"Oh, fuck," I gasp. "Oh, fuck, fuck, fuck, yes."

Ma'xon kisses me again. His tongue slides through my lips and I'm surrounded by his taste. I lick at his teeth, the sharp points a touch of danger that make me shiver, make me hunger for more. My hands move to cup his face, to keep him kissing me like this. I never want to breathe again if it means he stops. But when he pulls back, he takes his fingers with him.

"Lax, look at that pretty pussy," he groans. "Just one taste."

With an ease I can't understand, Ma'xon lifts me up and arranges me until he has my back pinned to a headboard.

The pillows beneath my ass raise me up to a perfect height for his mouth as he settles down between my legs. It's like he planned this moment with how perfect this bed is, helping to align our bodies for pleasure. His tongue is thick and long when he sweeps it through my folds. All the little taste buds rub against my clit until I'm practically screaming for more. It spreads more of that mating saliva over me until it drips between my butt cheeks.

"Ma'xon, oh my god," I moan, grabbing on his fin.

"The taste of you, Odette," he groans and looks up at me. "I want it every day and night until I am gone from this plane."

His eyes are dilated until I can't even see the grey of them. I'm lost in the wide black circles and leaning over to fall into them. How can he possibly be as lost to me as I am to him? A month of texts, a night of conversation, and he's ready to spend the rest of his life on his knees for my pussy.

I'm soaked and empty. His tongue flicks over my clit and there's a moment where I lose myself. Ma'xon works my body, holding me open for him while my fingers smooth over his fin, but my thoughts are somewhere else. My mind knows that my body has got this all covered. Whatever this feeling is, it's warm and soft, like someone had put filter glasses on me.

While everything he does to my pussy is heavenly, there is more to this. I see his hips grind into the bed, his need for pleasure so adamant, but not as important as mine. The way he touches me, in that gentle and caring way, melts my heart. The hand on my side that squeezes me in close yet is so tender. The other is underneath me, wrapped around my low back to support me.

This sounds just as crazy as being abducted by aliens, but the physical support he gives me feels like a look into the future. When the mating frenzy ends and the high fades away, Ma'xon will still support all of me. I know that whatever happens, he will keep me safe and will care for me.

The thought makes tears dribble down my face, a little cry stuck in my throat even though I'm fully aware that I'm coming again. I've never had such an out of body experience or so many orgasms in my life, and that is absolutely what I'm going to blame these emotions on.

"Daddy." A shudder of pleasure ripples through me when he kisses around my labia and mound. "Hold me, please."

He looks up and blinks, before I'm eased below him. Strong arms wrap around me and he coos in my ear. He holds me to his chest as a rush of emotions floods my system. I'm happy, at the beginning of the best life anyone could ask for, and I'm crying into my mate's chest.

"Odette, look at me, pup." He places a finger under my chin so we are looking at each other again. "What's got you crying like this?"

"It's just a lot," I sob. "I feel so good and so much. I can't make 'em stop."

A dry finger swipes across my cheek and Ma'xon rolls us onto our sides. He drapes a thigh over my hips when I make a noise at the shift. I don't want him to let go. The weight of him on me is the only thing keeping me from floating away. I want to bask in this attention, this caring and soft embrace. He makes another soft, almost babying sound at me.

"When I finished my training cycle for the program, they sent me your file. I didn't know what to expect," he admits. "You see so many success stories, or eventual successes, that you wonder if maybe yours will be the one that fails."

The hand on my chin moves to cup my cheek, his thumb rubbing over my temple. Goosebumps scatter across my shoulder when I think of our size difference, of how gentle he is with me.

"But I have never been more sure or excited for the future, for you to be in my life," Ma'xon says softly.

When I look into his eyes, I see the sincerity of this confession. He swallows hard, and even with his cocks pressed into my tummy, he's taking care of me first. I can't remember the last time I've been the first priority like this. It's like he'd rather walk over hot coals for me than be selfish.

I kiss his chest, mumbling my thanks into his skin as I do so. There is so much happening, but it feels simple. It feels like this is the path my life was always meant to be on. When I pull myself up higher to reach his neck, Ma'xon's hand moves down to my butt and squeezes. The size of it doesn't cover the full width of my cheek, but damn is that a full grab. A little whimper comes out of my mouth. It's the sort of pathetic noise I used to only make when I got wild in my self-care fantasies.

The one that is demanding, needy, and sensual all at once. I lick around his jaw and nibble at him, to show that despite my tears, I still know what I want.

"Odette," he starts anyway.

"This is a mating frenzy, Daddy, so mate me." My pout is more for effect than actual upset. I'm not going to let happy tears and big emotions ruin the dicking of my life.

"C'mere," he grumbles, before wrapping around me like he's a crescent roll and I'm a tiny weenie before rolling us over.

A squeal comes out of me at how fast we move, but now I'm on top. My legs are spread wide and when I roll my hips, arousal and spit smear across his torso.

"On your knees for me, pup," he commands.

This is a new voice, demanding but soft and one that has my eyes rolling back. This is better than my spank bank daddy fantasies. I want him to say everything to me in this tone, just so I can be a little turned on all the time.

I rise up as much as I can, eventually opting to get on one knee so I'm tall enough to arrange the bottom of his two cocks at my entrance. Ma'xon turns that navy shade again before he spits in his hands and strokes his cocks. I half bend over to watch because every time he does a down pull, his frills would tease my folds and I want more.

He does this a second time until he is slippery, but then his two fingers are back in his mouth. They come away just as shiny as his cocks before he smears it over my clit and around my pussy. I shiver as the sensation of it sets my skin on fire with need. My pussy aches, empty of his cocks.

And he has the audacity to finger me again.

"Just want to make sure you're ready." He grins, slowly fucking them into me like his dicks aren't right there.

"Fuck me, please." I rock my hips against his fingers. Their easy glide just makes me want to feel fuller. "I know my body, I want your cock in me, Daddy."

"Hold still for me then."

He grabs me by the waist with both hands and lifts. My knees are off the bed and Ma'xon shifts until his tail is over the edge. My fingers dig into his wrists as he starts moving me. My nonexistent abs tense to keep balance and so I don't fall face first into his belly.

"Hold the cock you want to ride for me, pretty girl," he says in that voice again.

I've never moved so fast in my life. I reach down in front of me and wrap my fingers around the base of the bottom cock. He grunts, his hips moving up on instinct to fuck into my fist. So he's needy too.

Good.

I take almost as much pleasure from that knowledge as I do when these frills slowly sink into me. Loose thoughts, I think, we need this to fit. He slowly lowers me down until we meet my fist around the base. I take my hand away and gravity does the rest.

My knees are spread wide again, my breathing is a bit laboured, and my fucking Christ do these frills feel good. Ma'xon raises his knees to support me, allowing me to lean against them in a way that means he is hitting a spot inside of me I have never imagined possible. My pussy won't stop pulsing, getting those frills to work my insides into producing more of my own arousal and relax my muscles.

"Sur'lax, you keep squeezing me, pup, and this is gonna get real messy real fast," he groans, even as he rocks me forward.

My oversensitive clit rubs against the space between his dicks and tears creep into my eyes again. It feels too good, I don't want it to end, but I'm struggling to even think straight. I look down at his top cock, how it nearly reaches my belly button and mewl. Where the fuck has this gone inside me? I let go of one of his wrists to wrap my hand around his other dick.

"So big." I press it into my tummy as I start moving with more intention. "Feels too good."

"No, you deserve this. Taking Daddy's cock so well, stretching your pussy for me? You deserve to feel good."

It punches the air right out of my chest. I do deserve this, and to feel sexy while I do it. Ma'xon grunts as I lean back against him, a dribble of lilac precum spreading across my belly. The cock in my hand twitches when I squeeze it. I look at his face, the navy flush and the sharp toothed snarl. His teeth are bared and there is more mating saliva threatening to spill out of his mouth.

I let go of his wrist to play with my nipples. They aren't my most sensitive sexy spot, but I know they look good. I know that when I pinch them a little too hard, they actually stay taut and perky. Ma'xon's eyes are glued to them as I rock on his cock. His hips jump and he lets go of my right side. The hand still holding me squeezes a bit harder. A vision of four sensitive bruises fills my head as I think about it.

"Yes," I moan. "Want you to mark me."

"Make yourself come on my cocks then, pup," he says.

With his free hand, he pushes up into a sitting position. I choke as the fullness inside me shifts. I think I feel his cock in my throat. I know that's impossible, but I'm willing to bet Ma'xon is capable of anything right now. He lowers his head to my free nipples and licks it.

"Oh, fuck."

Maybe this is one of my sexy spots when I'm stimulated right. Mating saliva spreads across my skin with each pass of his tongue. He drags his teeth against my flesh carefully as he does it. I move my hand to his fin again, holding him at my breast. He alternates between sucking and flicking at my nipple until I would announce in front of a judge that it was connected right to my clit.

Each time he teases the tip, my clit throbs. The longer this goes on, the longer my body refuses to finish. It's like I'm waiting for something more. I don't know what though, so I keep grinding my soaked pussy, moaning with a pleasure that won't peak.

Tears are slipping down my face again as desperation builds. I'm so close, my body wants to cross that finish line, but it's not happening. My muscles start to ache in a bad way. Even with his hand on my waist and his knees on my back, it's not enough.

"Ma'xon," I whine, hips slowing and sweat dripping heavily down the side of my face. "Help."

The look on his face is almost enough to reinvigorate me. Ma'xon looks downright unholy, like he wants to eat me alive.

"You tired, pup?" he asks, breathing a little heavy himself. "You need Daddy's help?"

"God-fucking-damnit," I mumble. "You're gonna kill me talking like that."

"Is that a good thing?" He moves his hips to meet my rocking, the slap of our skin echoing around the room.

"Yes, just fuck me like you really want to."

He grabs the back of my head and as we fall down together, smashes his mouth to mine. I'm flooded with the mating saliva, my body humming with the taste of sour apple. It leaks from my lips. There is so much of it and yet I want more, craving it like I need it to breathe. His tongue sweeps into my mouth, pushes back into my throat like he wants to make sure I'm as high as possible for what he's about to do to me.

With a cock in my pussy and one trapped between us, I'm only thinking about having another orgasm, and getting Ma'xon to cum. He promised me a mess and I won't be denied. He wraps his heavy arms around me, pinning me to his hard body. I'm smooshed and secure to him. Anticipation flutters in my tummy at what's going to happen next.

It's fast and deep. His strokes are hungry, that kind of selfish that I wasn't sure he was capable of, but I love it. My fingers curl around his shoulder so I don't bounce away, and he groans with every touch I give him. His thrusts grow powerful and demanding the more I caress his neck and chest. He fucks me with such a force that all words jiggle right out my head and into my mouth.

"Fuck, right there, yes Daddy, *please*, cum inside me," I scream against his chest.

"Shit."

The top of his thighs smack harder against my ass and my mouth falls open. Nothing but hiccupped moans and tears escape me. There's a hungry squelching sound each time he bottoms out and it sounds like the filthiest serenade a girl could ask for.

He cranes his neck until his teeth graze my shoulder. *Yes,* my body hollers at me, *yes.* There is no teasing or prep or questions. The tears in my eyes are from the release that he is going to give me. My desperation is going to end, he's going to get me over the edge.

Ma'xon bites me and the world explodes.

Chapter 8

Ma'xon

I CAN'T STOP. I don't stop.

Odette screams for me. The taste of her blood fills my mouth and her pussy squeezes my shaft so fucking hard I think it might break.

But Sur'lax, is this heaven? My tail flails against the side of the bed, and I'm thankful I had the sense to move it away from my pup. She's so squeezable and tender. I don't want to hurt her unnecessarily in my uncontrollable horniness. My cocks gush between us but my hips keep moving, fucking as much of it into her and onto her as possible.

I can't stop.

The mating frenzy closes off any thought of a respite. When I stop coming, my jaw unlocks and I let go. Blood and saliva smear her shoulder, but she snuggles into my chest, a sweet sound on her lips. She sounds so content, but we are only just getting started.

In a swift motion, I roll us over. She giggles and I'm hard as rock again. What in the Solarium has this human done to me already? I push up onto my forearms, my cock inside of her moving and the other twitching in the mess I have made on her stomach. I want to be deeper inside her, buried in her heart as much as her pussy. When I rock my hips more slowly to keep her loose and stimulated, she moans.

It's the sweetest sound.

My pup is wide awake after this bite. The extra mating saliva is doing its job to keep her loopy but lucid. She presses her thumb to the corner of my mouth, then sucks the mess clean with a smile. I don't stop moving, grinding my hips into her hot cunt while she licks her finger. Odette is everything I imagined and so much more. I'm in the tides of a frenzy, a low point after spilling inside her once, and she consumes my every thought still.

A tingling sensation shoots through me when she touches me again. If Axilarian had the ability to cry the way humans do, I would weep with happiness. Instead I'm lost in her eyes as she runs her fingers over my skin. Her touch is delicate, but there is a sure tenderness to it, like she knows that I crave her touch more than air.

I should have seen this coming.

Odette teases my gills and I thrust so hard she yelps. My jaw opens as a moan and saliva drip past my lips. Her body lurches toward the headboard and my cock nearly slips from her precious body. My noises turn feral at the thought of her trying to escape. She can't leave me. Not now, not ever.

"You wanna play, pup? We can play," I grunt as I peel myself away from her.

She pouts, reaching for me when I sit up on my knees. It brings me a sense of dark and male satisfaction to see this reaction from her. Just the tip of my cock sits in her wet pussy now. Our combined juices drip down underneath her, and I lean into the temptation. Sweeping up the mess between us with a finger, I bring it down to her asshole. Her breath hitches, but her body stays relaxed.

"Slow, Daddy, been a while," she cautions.

"Tell me if it hurts," I murmur in a soothing voice.

I lean forward to brush some of the hair from her brow, to simply touch her to let her know I will always be careful with her. She needs to drink more water, and in the back of my head I know I should get her what she needs. But her tiny little feet are planted on my calves trying to push herself back onto my cock. She wants me, not hydration. One more round, and I will do the decent thing of taking care of my mate.

With some teasing around her asshole, she opens up with slow, measured breathing. Her muscles are relaxed, but for extra measure, I pop my finger in my mouth again until it's coated in saliva. At the first touch, her body tenses, goosebumps run the length of her thighs, but then

Odette sighs. My finger eases into her ass, the rhythmic clenches pulling more and more of me inside her. It's torturing the head of my cock, the frills twitching and seeping juices around the opening of her pussy.

"Legs up for me," I say, voice straining as my need frays the edges of my control.

Carefully, she pulls her knees up toward her chest and raises her feet up. I wrap my arms over the top of her thighs, holding her calves to one side me, indulging in the feel of her bare skin on mine. My fingers dig into the plushness of her leg and I groan.

"You're so soft."

"Sorry," she says quickly, before sealing her lips shut like she didn't mean to apologise for the compliment I gave her.

"Don't be," I beg. "Please, don't ever be sorry for the way you are."

My hand smooths over her skin, feeling all the spots and hair. Odette is everything I could have ever wanted in a mate. I just know it. She needs to know it too.

With her thighs firmly pressed together, my finger in her ass, and my cock threatening to explode before I can even get us started, I arrange my top dick haphazardly to use her softness as a second pussy. She giggles when the frills touch her skin, but the sweet noise morphs into a gasp as I sink into her.

"How does it feel, pup?" I ask, muscles trembling as I hold still. Her grip on my cock is strangling, and I love it. My finger inside of her strokes upward against her walls just to tease her.

"So full, Daddy," she moans, her flushed skin glistening under the setting suns of Axilaria. "Like, like, I been missin' this."

"It's because we are meant for one another," I promise. Slowly, I ease out of her, trying to memorise the sounds of us together before I fuck my dicks back into my Odette. The slap of our skin is new music, still experimental and so free. "Just as we are, as the seas above have made us."

She nods, scooting herself deeper into the space between my spread knees. My finger slips deeper into her ass until my palm crowds against the space for my cock.

"*Fuck*," she groans. "Fuck me, please."

"Anything, pup."

I let the haze of the mating frenzy take over me. Our bodies clap together with each thrust of my hips. Her body shakes with the force of it until she has to grab her tits. Her small fingers pinch around her nipples until they are hard peaks. Odette's mouth is open, tongue resting on her bottom lips as she pants for air between screams of pleasure.

Saliva slips through my teeth. I don't try to stop it from coating the tip of my cock between her thighs. Every time it nudges against her belly, I think that will be the time that

I spill across her again. Her eyes are half closed, but they are directed right at my tip. She's watching me fuck her thighs.

"You see that?" I groan as her pussy begins to tighten. "These pretty thighs are Daddy's. Meant to be squeezed, and fucked, and loved on. Don't ever be sorry for that."

"Uh-huh, all yours Ma'xon," she mumbles.

It's my name on her lips. My body reacts like she has plucked it perfectly from the vine. My tail turns ridged before a jolt of energy shoots down to the tips. My cocks paint cum against her pussy walls and across her stomach. A splash of lilac against her red skin.

But she hasn't come yet. My cocks are still twitching when I throw myself back. I can't allow my mate to be deprived of pleasure I have allowed myself. She yelps when I wrap her slick thighs around my face. Her ass clenches around my finger as my mouth descends on to her swollen pussy.

Her body is warm and wet on its own, but the mess I have made of her makes my hearts stutter. Her flesh is swollen, smeared with our mixed arousal. Odette's pussy leaks so much of my cum, I can't hold in my groan of satisfaction. Every little fluttering of her hole pushes more of it out. I lick up our cum before thrusting my tongue back into her. With my free hand, I reach up to pinch her nipples just as she had done to herself. Her hand covers mine as she grinds her hips against my face.

As her legs begin to shake, her moans rise in pitch and breathiness. My finger still in her ass makes short, soft thrusts that pair with my tongue's deep dive into her wet pussy. Strings of profanity fall from her lips until she tenses. Her mouth, her voice, her body; they all stop their shaking and whimpering.

And then I am granted a most precious reward. Her pussy pulses around my tongue, juices mixing with my mating saliva. My teeth ache to sink into the meat of her thigh to prolong the ecstasy for her, but I resist. Her voice is a soft whimper when she speaks to me.

"Too much, Daddy."

Even mating saliva can only do so much to ease the over stimulation that frenzies produce. Carefully, I ease my finger from inside her ass before I scoop her up off my bed. There is no giggle this time when I carry her in my arms. Her skin is hot, her fingers trembling to hold on to my shoulder.

My blood is still pounding, my top cock still aches to be inside her. The odd thing is jealous of its counterpart as they wave around in the air with each step I take. But I have to provide for my mate. She needs me. And that beats fucking the frenzy out of me any day.

Once we arrive in the kitchen, I place Odette on the counter top. She hisses at the chill, but she doesn't question this change in scenery. I fumble around for a glass and the pitcher without looking away from her. Beyond not wanting her to fall, I don't want to miss a single moment with her.

She blinks slowly at me, a smile rising on her lips. My pup. My mate. The most beautiful flower on Axilaria has nothing on the content and well fucked look on her. Her short legs slowly adjust until she has exposed herself to me. It could be the mating saliva, it could be that elusive submissive state that was mentioned during our schooling.

Either way, my nostrils flare and I'm hit with the smell of us together. Deep breathing won't help calm my need, which seems to claw at all my actions now. I use my tail to flick the fridge door closed and pour the large glass for her.

Odette doesn't bring her hands to mine to take it. Instead her lip part, beckoning me to serve her. Like she already knows I can't refuse a single request from her. It gives me the opportunity to make her rehydrated though, and that's all that matters.

Her throat bobs until the glass is empty, droplets of water clinging to her lower lip.

"How was that, Daddy?" she asks, voice a little small and tired.

"You're doing so well for me, Odette." I tuck a piece of hair behind her ear and she leans into my palm. I'm utterly, happily lost in her. "Let's get you cleaned up some, then we can see about Daddy stretching your sweet pussy."

·♥·♥·♥·♥·♥·

There are moments when the frenzy sinks its teeth so deep into my consciousness, all I hear is Odette screaming with pleasure. My other senses turn off. My subconscious only wants the sweet music I can make my pup utter.

And it's beautiful.

I lose track of time, floating between kissing her, drowning her in me until she is nearly delirious, and slowly feeding her bits of fruit and glasses of filtered water. She lets me take care of her as much as she lets me use her body for our shared pleasure.

For the first time in days though, my cocks are soft and make no attempt to harden. My frills have stopped pulsing and are tucked beneath my foreskin. My body aches as well. The marathon mating has ruined my knees and back in a way that I relish.

We are plastered together, with Odette lying on top of me with sweat and cum holding us together. My hands hold her backside as she drools on my chest. We've only had short bursts of sleep since the start and this is the longest calm yet. I don't want to break this moment yet, but I know that we must clean up.

Or at the very least eat something truly nourishing that isn't sweet frenzy fruits the grocers sell to keep energies up during mating cycles.

That's another sign it's come to end. My thoughts have turned practical again. I can think of another being who isn't my mate. Still, I don't open my eyes, instead choosing to sink a bit deeper into the quietness of my thoughts and soft snoring from my pup.

I doze on and off, but finally my stomach protests loud enough that Odette wakes up.

"Hush timtum," she grumbles, her bottom lip poking out in a pout.

A smile creeps up my lips and I bring a hand up to scratch her scalp while she slowly wakes up. She groans into my touch, pushing her head into my palm. My Odette is a precious human, soft and giving when she wants to be and sassy other times that make something in me burn for her.

"We should have a shower, pup," I whisper, already shifting us out of bed with as little movement as possible.

"Yup," she sighs. "Then we sleep again."

"Then we eat some supper," I correct her. "We could both use something more hearty."

"Mmmm, would kill for a bacon, egg, and cheese," she mumbles.

"Those are breakfast foods, correct?"

"Yeah, on a bagel," she says.

"Breakfast for supper then?" I ask.

I don't know what a bagel is, but I will do my best to give her anything she asks for. She nods a little, but not much else, her arms draped around my shoulder but not really hanging on. Her complete trust that I will be able to carry us to our destination makes my chest warm. I was warned by the TRP that while my mating saliva will keep my human relaxed and horny for the duration of the frenzy, they would be incredibly exhausted once it wears off.

The bathroom lights slowly rise as we enter the room and we are blasted with fresh, floral air. The stench of five days worth of sweat and cum wafts through the air and we both turn up our noses. Odette's button nose is especially cute as it scrunches and pinches her features together. All romance of the before and the carnality of mating are gone. We are simply left with each other in the harsh reality of post frenzy clarity.

"I'm scared to separate," she says. "All my skin's gonna peel off."

I bark with laughter so hard my gills ruffle. She's *adorable*. I make quick work of turning on the shower unit and stepping under the hot stream though. We groan as our overworked bodies are pelted with the water. It slips down our skin and unsticks us enough that my pup can slide down my body without fear of being flayed. My cocks chub up at the slickness between us, but it doesn't last. With a hand on my arm to steady her, Odette turns around to face the water. She sighs in bliss and there is no minimising the glory of a hot shower on a sore and tired body.

I reach around us to grab the special body wash for her and lather up a huge dollop. Lazily, I scrub my mate from head to toe, making sure there isn't a speck of her I missed. This soap will help seal her skin to the humid air of Axilaria. It will still feel much like the hot jungle climates of Earth, but this will help her adjust. She is all soft noises while I work and it brings me a sense of joy.

Taking care of oneself is a chore, something we all must do to survive. But there is something extraordinary about what taking care of my pup does for me. By allowing me to do this, to take care of her, in this way and in any way she may want in the future, it gives me a sense of purpose that work never has.

She can do all these things herself. Odette is a capable adult, but in conversations leading up to our first meeting, it struck me how much she did for others. Even at the detriment to her own health, she would take on extra work for charity partners, volunteer with the local youth choir, and still find time to try and fix the broken house her father had abandoned. Rarely ever when I messaged, was she taking time for herself.

Now she would get all the time she could ever want. I would do anything for her within our means and realm if it brings a smile to her face. To see her light up with joy, not a touch of worry in her, makes my tail sway with pleasure. There will still be puddles for us to jump, but having Odette by my side is freeing and anchoring all at once.

"Your soap doesn't smell like you," she says, rinsing the slippery hair conditioner out.

"What should it smell like?" I ask. If my mate wants me to smell a certain way, I will do my best to achieve it.

"Lightening." Her hair squelches as she squeezes the ends. "A stormy ocean."

"Very poetic of you." I smirk as she sticks out her tongue. "But generally soaps here smell like flowers or fruit."

"But your aftershave didn't."

Then it dawns on me, the scent she likes some much is the sweet rillin oil. As soap washes off my body, it is replaced with smug satisfaction. So not only did she pick up the smell, she misses it now even out of a mating frenzy. I will have to find an everyday oil to use for her.

"Well, if you like the way that smells I can buy something with it then. That oil is special," I say, curling around her until her plump backside rubs against my thighs. "For mating."

"God, I can't think about mating for like two days, maybe three. My body is too tired to be turned on."

I smile and kiss her shoulder. "Understandable, pup. Let's get some food in your belly."

Chapter 9

ODETTE

AXILARIAN BAGELS ARE THE *shit*. Like I could have eaten fifteen of the breakfast sandwiches Ma'xon made for us. Which is saying something since it contained no pig or flour. Most meat products on the planet are fish based, with the occasional poultry delicacy. I'm glad he told me all this after we had started eating. There was no seafood taste to my sandwich at all though. It tasted like the bagel sandwiches I love getting at home.

Thinking of home now makes me a little sad. Not in a way that makes me want to go back, but I do wish I could have grabbed my favourite stuffed animal, Marbles, before being whisked off my feet. Maybe I'll be able to find something like it here, but for now all I've got is Ma'xon's big hand in mine as we walk towards the shopping concourse for the colony.

The two suns of Axilaria shine through the liquid sky overhead. The buildings around us are coated in the reflection, like we are standing in one massive underground aquarium. That is why the planet is so humid and why the people have gills, I guess. We are all swimming standing up as we go about our days.

"How do you tell them apart if everyone just calls their hometown their colony?" I ask, trying to subtly watch people. There are a lot of different kinds of aliens around, with plenty of humans in the mix. Even a giant, sentient church gargoyle who is carrying an arm load of new beach gear with a human holding onto his tail so they don't get separated.

"Technically they have names, like this is Colony-3Q4S, but that title is really only used for tourist and senate meetings. We are a small peaceful world, and we all share this floating space rock as our home."

"That sounds very idyllic," I say.

"You'll get used to it," he promises with a squeeze to my fingers. "How about we start with bathing suits since you seem very keen on swimming?"

We've stopped in front of a giant shop front that appears dedicated to off-planet swim gear. Like every other building, we need to climb stairs to enter and it's all built out of something that kind of reminds me of decking. It's not wood or brick, but some kind of plastic. As we enter, there are a few others milling about, but it's generally quiet. Ma'xon points to a sign above us.

"Second floor for humans," he reads. "Oh, and for dry gear. We're on the same level then."

I try to keep my expectations low. I love shopping, I have since I was a preteen, but the accessories and the shoes can only be so interesting after watching your friends walk into the change rooms with enough clothes to fill a closet. What do Axiliarian's expect of human clothes? Let alone bathing suits?

Ma'xon guides us through narrow racks that hold lit glass frames of clothes. Each frame holds a new wetsuit, a small screen above them displaying the variety of colour they come in. Oh, this is *bougie*. But I don't know if I would call scuba equipment a bathing suit. I narrow my eyes at the giant shark man holding my hands. He's wearing a fitted tank top deal with equally fitted leggings that have a cord around his tail. Around the sides of his shirt is mesh so his gills can breathe. It's not exactly a wetsuit, but it's definitely not what I'm used to wearing.

Even my outfit today isn't the same as his. I'm dressed for gym class circa the sixties. This morning, Ma'xon presented me with this romper that is made of thin, faded cotton and buttoned up the front. The last human to come to this colony wanted me to have this, apparently. It fits like a glove and my mate couldn't take his eyes off my legs the whole tram ride here.

Thank god the body lotion here is anti-chafing.

"I'm not sure how much of selection they'll have," Ma'xon murmurs, leaning down a bit to be closer to me. "But I know another colony that is much more human centric we can visit sometime."

I take a deep breath, still finding the piercing in my nose a bit tickly. How many humans have been mated to aliens? Obviously, I'm not the first, but my curiosity skyrockets at the idea that there's a colony that has constructed itself around humans more than Axilarians. Maybe that colony had one of the first abductees.

Is that the right word? I mean I was taken from earth without my knowledge. But if I'm fine with it does that make it okay? Or was agreeing to being mated to an alien buried in the terms of service I didn't read? Either way, I don't feel like a victim of a crime. I feel like I won the fucking lottery.

"Odette?"

"Sorry," I say quickly as heat rises up my cheeks. "I'm sure we'll find something, and I'm used to stores not having my size."

"Everything is made to fit, pup, that's not the problem. I want you to find things you love."

My heart flutters a little as the thought of shopping till my arms ache and the bags that line them leave permanent marks on my skin. "You're really gonna regret saying that."

Ma'xon smiles at me and stops us in the far back corner of this level. In front of me is a rack of two dozen different bathing suits and wetsuits. From speedos to full coverage wetsuits with head coverings, there has to be a style of swimwear for just about everyone. My eyes snag on a slinky string bikini style, and a big hand lands on the display screen to swipe through the colourways for it.

"Red?" He nods.

"I'm gonna look like a fire truck," I pout.

"The sexiest and most adorable fire truck," Ma'xon agrees. "What other styles do you want? I won't barge in again."

I don't think he knows what a fire truck really is, but I select three more suits, two of which are a classic one piece fit and then a knee length wetsuit just because that seems to be the norm. Then a small bell dings overhead.

An Axilarian waves us over, smiling extra wide when Ma'xon turn around with me.

"You can head right through those doors, machine's all ready for ya," he says.

I step through the frosted sliding doors, trying to figure out if by machine he means that I'll have to get my measurements scanned or something. I don't know how space clothes are made, but I assume there's something like that. Except I'm alone when I twist around to ask.

I poke my head through the door again and I see the two men are in deep conversation about something. Ma'xon scratches the bottom of his fin while the other guy's tail starts to sway more aggressively the longer they are talking.

I give them a few more minutes, but when they are still not done, I turn back to the dressing room.

Nested in each pale blue cubicle is a shower head and bank atm. Is this so I can test the suits and pay for them automatically? There haven't been any exchange unions here even if I did have cash on me. Then, a soft, feminine voice nearly scares the shit out of me.

"Please step under the holo-array to be fitted."

The shower overhead turns on and blue light rains down from it. I have no reason not to trust it, but I only put in the tip of my busted ballet flat. Nothing happens. Not to me or the machine. It doesn't even make a sci-fi-y noise when I dip my foot out and in again. Once I step under the light, a ring of green light flows down from before it completely dims.

That is all it takes to do my full measurement?

I turn around to the atm and see a full 3D model of my body on screen. Fuck me. I'm not horrified at all with what's on screen. In fact the first thing that comes to mind when I see it is that my ass looks amazing. Generally, I feel pretty neutral about my body. But seeing this digital version of me with that fire truck red bikini on makes me think I'm fine as all get out. Just like a smartphone, I can pinch the screen here and zoom on the design.

Before I can move on to the next one, I have to approve each colour first. After seeing how great the red looks, I change the next suit from a plain navy to a black and white pin stripe pattern that makes the model look curvier and taller. On the third suit, I go bold and make it a royal purple colour. I leave the more practical suit black just so I have a basic piece.

Then the machine starts to hum. In less than a minute a medium sized pouch pops out of the atm. Clearly labelled 'compostable' in the top with a barcode to scan at the bottom. That happens three more times before I have all of my custom made clothes.

I rush out of the cubicle to find Ma'xon. He is right where I left him, still talking to the guy. With one arm full of bags, I can only grab him a little bit but it works. I squeeze his side hard. This was utterly life changing, even more so than finding out humans aren't alone in the universe.

Clothes are made exactly to fit my body.

"Look, Der'lo, you know I'm not really the one who takes care of this anymore."

"Yeah, yeah," he says, but from his tone I don't think he gets it. "Let me ring you up, so you can get outta here."

This part of our shopping experience is extremely normal. But the thrill of walking out of the store with a bag full of clothes isn't lost on me. My chest feels lighter. It's like some fear that I was used to hanging over every aspect of my daily life has finally been lifted. I can see the world and my place in it with a different potential now.

"That was so fucking amazing, can we keep shopping?" I ask. When I look up, Ma'xon is grinning from ear to ear. All his shark teeth are showing and I just think I could kiss him until I pass out.

"Of course, pup." He takes the bag from my wrist and wraps his free arm around my shoulder. "You've got a whole closet to fill."

I never understood the shopping addiction thing. If anything I'm firmly a person who gets buyer's remorse. That odd guilt from spending money that knots up my stomach until I return whatever I've bought. Many trips to the mall back home were spent hyperventilating in my car, rationalising that I did in fact need a new pair of jeans because the single pair I owned had a thigh seam blow out.

But today, I have none of that remorse. Not a single drop of it. Every time a clerk rings us up, Ma'xon taps a clear screen device that's about credit card size to till and asks me if I'm sure that's all I want. As if the bags and bags of clothes weighing his arms down aren't a burden, or too much spoiling. He kept insisting if I like the design of something, I should get it in all the colours I like.

Axilarian clothes are all humidity proof, with lots of mesh panelling to allow gills to breathe. I spend a whole three seconds deciding that I don't care if I look pale. I'm living on a planet that is always hot, I'm gonna show some skin. A regular outfit here consists of a few pieces, kind of like on Earth. Tops, bottoms, sandals; totally regular stuff you'd buy to fill your closet.

I'm glad I didn't have to try these on in store either. I don't want Ma'xon to miss out on seeing the fashion show. Which he would have at every store we were at this afternoon. At least one person would stop him to ask about something to do with the colony or an upcoming senate hearing. He'd nod at me to silently tell me to go pick out what I want, and only when I was ready to check out did people finally get the message to stop chewing his fin off about work he has retired from.

They know he *is* retired, right?

"I vote," he murmurs, leaning over so the other passengers on the tram don't overhear us, "that when we get home, we order in for dinner. I introduce you to the best movie of all time. Then late night swim."

I purse my lips, pretending like I am thinking very hard about what sounds like a perfect evening to me. "Do we get dessert?"

"If I ever say no to dessert, I need you to hang me out to dry," he says.

Eagerly, we launch into a discussion about what the best desserts are and I'm happy to forget about anyone else existing. When we arrive back home, there is a small basket overflowing with flowers and a small invitation. I carry it into the kitchen while Ma'xon drops my shopping in the bedroom.

"To the happy couple, love Pri'za," I shout. "P.S. Drag Ma'xon to lunch on Cortus so the three of us can get to know one another."

I hear the groan almost instantly, and my mate sustains the long drawn out noise until he has me pressed into the counter.

"What's Cortus?"

"Like Tuesday, it's just a day of the week," he says.

"So why are you groaning about lunch with your sister?"

"Because she will want to talk about politics." He nuzzles into my shoulder, kissing the one lingering bite mark I have from the frenzy. "Her mate, Al'dren, has a very firm 'no work outside of business hours' policy."

"I mean..."

"Yes, it's very good of him, isn't it?" Ma'xon teases, tickling my sides until I'm wiggling myself onto the counter top. "Now, let me introduce you to the Axilarian version of Thai food."

We order enough food to feed a small army. There are towers of metal takeaway bowls called tiffin tin stacked up around us. Apparently those are a traditional Indian lunch box that Axilarians have adapted. After we wash them, we set them outside for someone to collect in the morning. If it weren't for our leftover noodles tucked away into the fridge, it would be like we'd never eaten.

The taste of new fruit is still on my lips. For dessert, we ordered some kind of sweet fruit filled Jell-o that looked more like art and less like food. Watching Ma'xon's sharp teeth cut through it was almost heartbreaking, but once it was ruined I was happy to dive in. The exact fruit comparison escapes me, but I could have eaten a whole one of those all by myself.

As the miles on end credits roll, it doesn't escape me how domestic everything feels. I've been on an alien planet for a week, with most of that time being spent in bed having endless amounts of orgasms. With Ma'xon, it's easy to slip into the groove of it all. Laying here on the couch with my legs draped over his lap is what I dreamed about at home. This natural affection and cohabitation.

I want to spend the next twenty-five years, at least, doing this. Maybe not shopping everyday because that's insane, but doing activities together without stress. I don't want either of us to have to stress about deadlines or needing to be somewhere else. Our focus should just be on the pleasure of each other's company.

"How ya feeling?" I ask him.

"Full," he responds quickly, as the projector screen on the wall begins its ascent. "Why did I let you order so much food?"

"Me?" I laugh. "No one said you needed to get three appetisers."

"Pssh, second best part of dinner, after dessert."

"No, it's all about the noodles." I try to reach a hand to his side to tease him, but my arm is too short. "Help me up so I can push you."

"C'mere, pup."

He leans over, his arm slipping behind my back and then he scoops me up. I yelp as he stands up, my limbs flailing around to grab hold of him. "Do you think I'd drop you?"

"Not on purpose."

"I'm so offended," he gasps. "Look at these strong arms."

He curls me like I don't weigh more than a can of soup, rising and lowering until it feels like I might fall. Each time he does it my belly swoops like I'm on a rollercoaster. Giggles burst out of me even more when each time I get close to his face, he kisses me wherever he can reach me.

Then I'm falling.

Me and the waterbed jiggle and that all too familiar giddiness takes over me. The desire to be playful with my partner and enjoy the freedom this new life affords me. Ma'xon grabs my ankles and starts nibbling at me until I'm squealing with delight. In an amazing show of waterbed physics on my part, I bounce and wrap my leg around his torso, pulling him down onto me while he's distracted.

"Okay," I say, trying to catch my breath.

He looks down at me, grey eyes sparkling. He seems less stressed now, in a genuine way that was missing this afternoon. He was trying to hide it, but now it's finally melted away. He's playful too.

"Feels like we should just stay in bed," he whispers.

I wrap my other leg around his middle. His cocks rub against me, half hard and I'm flooded with the memory of how good they feel inside me. Besides my feet from walking today, I'm not sore. His body pressed against mine just makes me feel needy for more.

"But then you won't get to see me in that bikini, Daddy." I kiss the corner of his mouth, his jaw, purposefully avoiding his mouth.

"Pool time," he announces, swiftly rolling off me. "Get dressed while I get it set up."

His tail is practically wagging as he leaves, and all I can think about is that I'm going to bone in a pool for the first time.

Chapter 10

Ma'xon

I HEAD OUT TO the back porch and my shoulders slump. I'm not making a good first impression. A real impression not based on our mating frenzy. This is Odette's chance to see our colony, our planet, and I fumbled in our first outing impeccably. How could I let everyone pull me into conversation after lengthy conversation about issues that haven't been my problem over a cycle now.

I am retired. I say the phrase to myself several more times. My mate is supposed to be my main focus. It's why I handed over power. Pri'za is the leader of this colony. If there are concerns about uneven paving stones, they are her problem now. Yet I stood there like a lemon, listening to all of them.

And my mate shopped without me. I was just the baggage collector at the end of the day. She stood there each time, waiting for people to introduce themselves, waiting for them to leave so we could have our day together. It was only when I could tell they weren't going to be done expressing their concerns for our community that I had to signal her on. I want her to have all the things she needs here. My former role shouldn't hinder that.

She didn't complain once and I wish she had. Her comfort and care are more important to me. A slight frown on her lips would have been all it took for me to overpower my long held sense of responsibility. I know my mother ran the colony until well into her 100s, but that isn't how I want to spend that last third of my life. I want to spend it with my mate.

Who wants to go for a swim.

My resolve to be better reinstated, I swing the door to the pool shed open and get it running. To my right, the deck floor begins to recede. The lights under the water slowly change from blue to purple to indicate it's maintaining a stable temperature. The swimming jets turn on, but I'm quick to cancel that command. We aren't working out.

This is to relax and spend quality time with Odette.

I strip out of my clothes and step into the refreshing water. On the far side there is a built-in bench that I don't intend to leave until my gills have turned pink. We need to ease our worries and sore feet.

The moon is bright tonight, nearing its fullest phase. Ours is much like Earth's, but it's harder to see here. The thick, liquid atmosphere surrounding Axilaria kept us safe from invasion until we were ready to explore the solar system. That was aeons ago now, yet having seen it and other moons in all their glory, I wonder sometimes if we are missing out on something.

Will Odette find it lacking in some way?

My fear that she will find this place subpar compared to her old life still sneaks its way into my thoughts. She is my mate for Sur'lax's sake. If she did not want to be here with me, it would have been decided before the frenzy. Before she even asked me if I would go home with her. The deck creaks and I look towards the door. Odette walks out onto the deck and any thought of her leaving melts away.

She's stunning. She's grabbed a towel from the bathroom, but she hasn't wrapped it around herself. All her curves are on display, with her little tan lines making her skin glow in that bright red swimsuit. My jaw drops. I think it will every time I see her dressed in clothes from our colony. Her eyes are stuck to me in the water.

Do I look like a predator to her? It was something they warned me about during training. Some humans have a fear of this carnivorous fish species that roam different oceans on Earth. My tail twitches, the water around me moving and that breaks her focus.

She drops her towel next to my clothes and stands at the edge of the pool.

"How deep is it?"

"It comes up to about my shoulders," I answer. My understanding of human imperial measurements is weak. The metric system is much easier to learn, but we don't use it here so I'm out of practice for that as well.

My Odette smiles and takes a step back. She launches herself off the deck and curls into a ball. Her splash washes over me in a tall wave. As I sputter for air, her laughter breaks the quiet of the night. It warms my hearts, makes them beat that little step harder.

While she swims in lazy circles around the middle of the pool, I go back to admiring her. Thinking about how lucky I am to have found my mate in a being so carefree, or at least someone who I could help reveal this carefree side of them. She only mentioned it once, but during our 'talking' phase it slipped she didn't do many things for fun.

"How do you have so much energy, pup?" I tease, snagging her around the waist when she swims near me.

"I'm just excited to have a pool." Her arms wrap around my neck, little fingers stroking the base of my fin. "Ya know, this is how you know you made it. You've got a private pool."

I pause for a moment, trying to think of how there could be a place where even small swimming pools weren't required for a house to meet living standards. "Did you not have one?"

"Oh lord no," she chuckles.

My fingers twirl around the strings of her bikini, the little bits floating around her hips begging to be pulled apart. It would be so easy. My cocks begin to harden, slowly growing to fill the space between us.

"A tragedy," I say, leaning in to kiss her cheek.

"A crime," she agrees.

Her head drops to the side, exposing her neck. My teeth scrape across her skin, but I don't know who it's teasing more. Me or her? A little nibble and her hips jerk against me.

"Daddy," she mumbles.

One of her hands travels down to my chest. Those deft little fingers smooth across my side and massage my gills. She pulls a moan from me like we have been mates for decades. Already so at ease with touching the parts of me that don't match her. My skin tightens and the tips of my fins tingle with the joy of her hands on me. I hug her closer to me, her soft little body giving and precious. This is my everything. If I never saw anyone again, I know I would be happy with just my Odette.

"You okay?" she asks, pulling away to look into my eyes.

Those little green rings are dark puddles I could fall into when I look at my mate. How do I explain the bone deep feeling of completeness she gives me?

"I'm better than okay," I promise. "Just thinking about how lucky I am."

"You're about to get luckier," she giggles and then her crass little joke dawns on me.

"That was terrible."

"Well you didn't bring me to outer space to make jokes," she laughs even harder. Every little bounce makes her chest shake, nipples pressing through the small triangles.

"No." I smile. "I did it so I can spoil you, pup."

"You've done a very good job of it so far." She kisses the space between my nostrils. "Let me thank you."

Her hand leaves my gills, dancing through the water until her small fist wraps around my top cock. She can't get her hand around one of them, but another time, I'm going to ask her to try holding both at once. Just so I can see the size difference between us, see how obscene it is that one of my dicks can even fit inside her. A firm grip with her soft hand is all it takes for me to be achingly hard. She strokes me slowly, not taking her eyes off me.

"Only if you want," I insist at the last minute.

Sexual favours aren't why I want to spoil her. I would do it everyday for the rest of our lives even if she never wanted to have sex again. She is mine, and that is enough to have me wanting to take care of her every need. No thanks required.

"I don't want it." I tense and she kisses my mouth softly. "I need your cocks, Daddy."

I slam my mouth to hers. Thank Sur'lax. Relief floods me when she smiles into our kiss. My tongue plunges into her mouth, and all I want is to taste all over her again. Have her spread those thick thighs for me every meal time so I can feast on her pretty pussy. That is what I need.

Odette lets go of my cock to move to my hands. I grip her hips hard, grinding her on my lap when she stops touching me.

"Take them off," she whimpers.

Seas above yes. I tangle my fingers into the string and tug until they are swimming around us. The material slips between us and floats off. There is no breaking our kiss to worry about them. I slide the triangles of her top to the side to free her breasts.

She moans when I lift her up. Her nipples tighten in the humid air. The little peaks are just visible, the light around us making her skin glisten. I wrap my lips around one and suckle. This foreign sensation does something to my insides. These are unlike anything I have experienced before and I believe I am obsessed with them.

Her little noises, praise, and encouragement make it all the more favourable. My eyes close to bathe in the sound of her voice. She enjoys it when I do this, especially when my teeth get close to the dark circles that surround them. I will do whatever it takes to please my mate.

"Yes, Daddy, feels so good." Her voice rises in pitch when I flick my tongue across her nipple.

My hand moves from her hip to spread her ass cheeks. She drips with more than pool water. The scent of her arousal mixes with the air and satisfaction washes over me. The frills of my cocks are threatening to burst from their sheath, but I don't care. I move my grip so my fingers can tease her pussy open.

Her juices cling to her flesh in a way the water doesn't. Odette bucks her hips when I nudge her little clit. That sensitive part of her drives her more crazy than my gills do to me. It's a pleasure spot that demands my attention. Her body reacts to the slightest touch of it, her skin heating and muscles tensing like it commands her.

My finger plunges into her pussy. She knows me, craves me now like I crave her. Her body gives under my advances as I push deeper into her. Her slick pussy grips onto me with each stroke. She doesn't want to let me go but each time I fuck it back inside of her a little more arousal drips onto my hand.

"More," she demands.

I look up at her. Her face is flush again, almost like it was during the mating frenzy.

"What do you want, pup?" I ask.

"Both." She grinds her pussy onto my finger. "Want both your dicks inside me."

I swallow. It was something we didn't manage during our first cycle. There is no reason for me to press for it, and I assumed we'd try it during our next one. But my mate looks at me with such determination and insistence that I'm concerned I will spill prematurely.

"I, uh," she starts to speak, but then shifts gears.

She sinks back into the water so her knees are spread wider across my lap. My finger slips from her pussy, but then she reaches behind us to move my hand where she wants it. I watch my mate twist with a tiny grunt, but then she seats herself on my finger again. Her ass gives little by little until I am knuckle deep in her.

She sighs, laying her head on my chest. "I did a bit of prep before I came out."

Sweet Sur'lax, this is my mate? This precious being is all mine? I kiss her forehead tenderly, but she is a needy thing tonight. Odette fucks herself slowly on my finger. Each time her warm cunt grinds on my cocks until I am panting along with her in an effort to control myself.

My gills flutter when her hands grip right underneath. She is close to touching them, but the tease makes this so much better. Her arms press her tits closer together, jiggling every time she humps my hand. This isn't about me, this is my mate taking pleasure from me, but seas above she's beautiful. I can't take my eyes off of her. Just like I promised her, I want to spoil her in every way.

"More?" I ask, lowering my head to nibble at her throat like she likes.

"One at a time," she requests, rising up just enough for my top dick to nudge at the entrance of her pussy.

"Tell me if it's too much, Odette. This isn't like the frenzy."

"Really?" She grins at me. "'Cause I feel like I'm about to lose it if you don't let me bounce on your cocks."

My cheeks heat. I don't understand why but her speaking like this makes me feel scandalised and dirty. That is the point, I know, but my thoughts turn hazy either way. Two can play this game.

"Then take what's yours, pup. Show Daddy what you can do."

She's quick, even with my finger keeping her ass stretched. Her hands wrap around me and she sinks down cautiously. It's fun to play, but she is taking care of herself too. As the head of my cock slips into her pussy, the foreskin pulls back and my frills are finally free. They splay open and a spurt of precum lubricates the rest of the way for her to sink down on me.

"Oh." She inhales. "Oh, fuck."

"How's that big cock feel?" I tease, tensing so I twitch inside her.

"Like it's mine," she groans. "Jesus, this—Daddy—"

Her body shivers as she rises up. The clutch of her pussy threatens to end me. It's wet and hot and mine. I pull my finger from her ass so only the tip fills her. She whimpers, that bottom lip of hers popping out like she's upset with how empty she now is.

But it doesn't last. She drops back down onto my lap in one smooth motion. Odette grunts, mouth forming a small O shape. She keeps doing this, using me, torturing me with pleasure as the water quakes and threatens to spill over the edge. Her urgency rises rapidly, showing me how close she is to tipping over the edge as well.

"Cum for me, pup. Like this, then you'll take both of me," I promise.

I must keep it, I must last, yet I'm desperately clinging on to my own control. I want to lift us up, lay my mate down on the deck and fuck her until all she can do is scream for her Daddy. She is so close to oblivion as it is, her head bobbing up and down the only response I get to my request. My tail tingles as her pussy starts to pulse around me.

She cries out a choked sound as her thrusting stutters. My hips surge forward to stay surrounded by that wondrous tight heat of her cunt. Her grip at my sides is almost bruising, but slowly they slide over my stomach and up my chest. She kisses my neck softly.

"So good for me, pup, such a sweet little mate," I praise her, smoothing my free hand over her back. "Do you want to keep going?"

"Yes, please," she says, and I feel her smile against me.

"I'm going to pull my finger out. Can you help Daddy?" I kiss her shoulder before she slowly lifts herself off my lap. "Good girl, now spread your cheeks for me."

Her hands leave me and I almost regret this instruction. Odette leans forward, using me to balance as she takes each of her glorious ass cheeks in hand and spreads herself open for me. She shivers when my finger leaves her hole, but she isn't empty for long.

I line my bottom dick up with her, pressing in just the tip. With a few strokes, I leak precum just inside her entrance. Her impatience returns quickly, rocking back and forth in short succession to spread more of my lubrication inside her.

Her body gives so easily to mine. My tail flicks, a rippling in the water that has me pushing forward more than I intended to. She moans a long, drawn out sound that makes me freeze.

"Daddy, more."

"Deep breath."

There is a pause. I listen to my mate take a round of measured breaths and then I guide her back down on my cocks. My fingers shake with tension around her waist, threatening to grab and fuck her harder than I want to right now. I want this first time for us to be perfect. Her body sinks into mine with an amount of work. With a few pauses to adjust to the girth of my cock stretching her ass, Odette finally sits fully.

It's a divine experience. My body floats off into our atmosphere to swim with our ancestors. Her eyes flutter closed as her lips part. She lets go of her ass, and the tightness around the base of my cock intensifies. I shift us closer to the edge of the bench so my feet sit firmly on the floor.

"Oh god," she groans.

Her hands are shaking too.

She leans back and grabs my face. I am stunned by the tears in her eyes again. Is she in pain? My chest tightens at the very thought. It's the last thing I could ever want. I raise my hand to cup her cheek, thumb brushing away an errant drop of wetness.

My worry must be written on my face. Her lips collide with mine, little tongue teasing me until I let her invade my mouth. Slowly she begins to grind against me. Sparks shoot off behind my eyes and vibrate all of my fins. I can't imagine a better feeling. Her body rocks against mine and I'm happy to perish this way.

Until she finds the confidence to thrust.

Odette comes off my dicks only a few centimetres. It is barely anything and yet the slide of her on my shafts sends me into a tailspin. I gasp for air.

"Use my cocks," I moan, moving my hand to grip her thighs. "Fuck yourself like the needy little pup you are Odette."

She licks her lips. Those little hands go back to the spot just beneath my gills.

"Lean back a little," she says, hooking her feet on top of my thighs.

I do as my mate requests, and I am rewarded with a surreal experience.

Over her shoulder, beneath the rippling surface of the pool, I watch her arch. Her stretched holes bend the known universe and my cocks as she flicks her ass up. She curls back slowly, testing the movement for accuracy while I am about to bite through my tongue. My fingers dig into her hips and she pauses.

"Is this okay?" she pants, looking up at me with lust written across her face.

"I can't describe how good this feels," I say. If she had done this during a frenzy I would have drowned in my own mating saliva. This is the most intense suction and pleasure my body has ever experienced. A wicked little grin spreads across her face.

Odette pops her ass in that same motion again, fast and without end. My hips don't even have time to thrust to meet hers. The frills on my cock stiffen, my tail is rigid. The water around us rises in increasingly taller waves just like my orgasm. The tidal wave of my pleasure is threatening to crash into me.

I open my mouth to warn her to slow down, but all that comes out is a moan.

"Is that good, Daddy?" she whimpers, breathing heavily. "Are you gonna come inside me?"

My hearts stop. She throws her ass back one more time and I explode. Like she can feel me spilling my soul into her body, she bears down hard on my cocks to lock us together. My tail thrashes, splashing the both of us. Odette's little laugh makes her clench harder, and my cocks dribble out more cum until at last, I am emptied.

It takes a moment for me to realise what I've done. The euphoria of being completely inside my mate overwhelms me until my cocks have softened inside her. She hasn't moved, they are still tucked neatly into each of her holes. Her finger petting my chest brings me back to my senses.

"You didn't—"

She stops me with a kiss.

"Sorry, pup," I whisper anyway.

"No apologies." She frowns at me, cupping my cheek like I had her. "Sex isn't about keeping score for one. And for two, I'm getting sore on my knees and wanna change location to bed."

I hug Odette. All the muscles in my body feel loose and are buzzing with the chemical release that comes with an orgasm. She kisses my shoulder and neck while we cuddle. This is what it means to have found a mate, I realise. This warmth that fills my chest and weight that is lifted off my shoulders just by being near her. She doesn't need to do anything, but be herself and already she has stolen my hearts.

Carefully, so my cocks stay snug inside her, I carry us out of the pool. My own knees wobble when I am on the deck again and she giggles at me. I can't see her swim bottoms anywhere in the water, so I will have to hunt them down in the morning.

"Hold tight," I say, right before I bend over to grab our stuff.

She makes a quiet noise of surprise but holds the towel and pile of clothes I give her. I try to close up the pool quickly. For good measure, I fish out a cleaning tablet and hand the puck to Odette.

"Toss it in and see what happens."

She lobs it, barely making it over the edge with her hands full, but it works. The water begins to boil, turning a neon green colour. Then in a blink it's back to normal.

"Damn, that cleaned the whole pool?"

"Yup," I say, flicking switches to finish shutting it all down.

"Heckon space, man," she mutters, but the lazy grin on her face tells me she isn't the least put out like she was my pants.

"Heckon space."

Chapter 11

Odette

Time flies when you're having fun. It also goes by at the speed of light when you no longer have to keep track of what day it is. I've convinced my body that I no longer have to wake up early and be stressed. Teaching my brain is taking a bit longer, but it's a work in progress. If it weren't for waking up with my period today, I'm not sure I ever would have realised it had been nearly a month since I came to Axilaria.

Light streams through the loose weave curtains, the breeze causes the red flowers—Ialots— wrapping around the beams overhead to rustle, and a cramp that could topple an empire seizes my lower tummy. As I tuck my legs into a foetal position, I can feel the mess in my pyjamas. Living in my dream fantasy world never included this aspect of reality. I take a few deep breaths, cycle breathing through the pain, but it doesn't help. This definitely proves humans can't mate outside of their species. That fear lasted all of two seconds after the frenzy, but you never know. I could have been the next virgin Mary. Of space.

I squeeze the blob shaped pillow tighter into my chest. Another tragedy of Axilaria, there are no stuffed animals. Kids just don't have them apparently, and despite great expeditions around the shopping district, nothing is the same. Marbles is the thing that I miss most about Earth. He wasn't the prettiest teddy bear these days, but he never let me down.

"Morning, pup." Ma'xon kisses my forehead, but he doesn't linger in bed. "I've got a meeting in few, but I want to have breakfast."

And increasingly often, my giant shark man has been getting out of bed earlier and earlier for *meetings*. So there is nothing for me to cuddle on while I try to wake up.

"Kill me," I grumble, burying my face in the subpar pillow.

There is a beat of silence before I hear it. Ma'xon takes a deep breath and I know his cute little nostril slits flutter a little. He pulls the sheet from my body and I don't even react. That's how bad the cramp is.

"I'm calling the practitioner," he says. This is the most urgent I think he's ever sounded.

And to be perfectly honest, some space drugs would be great right now to relieve this pain. Then he's gone for a few minutes. I can hear his tail knocking against the hallway, but not the actual words. He must be really agitated. Maybe this is the one thing he didn't learn at the TRP mating school. Which would really be saying something because that place knows more about humans than most humans even know about themselves.

"Daddy," I groan as I sit up. "I'm okay."

"I'm pushing my meeting back," he says, rushing back into the room to kneel in front of me. "What can I do to help?"

"I just need a hot shower and mountain of drugs to last the next few days." I rub the sleep from my eyes and toss the pillow to the side. He looks at it with a frown. "I'm really okay."

"The practitioner said she would have your tincture ready later this afternoon. Do you want to try out the dry spa today to help relax?" His hands move up my thighs and around my back. Heavy fingers knead my low back while he looks at me with the most caring and guilty grey eyes.

"Yeah, it sounds great," I sigh as muscles begin to heat and relax. "Are we still gonna have breakfast?"

"Of course."

Ma'xon scoops me up and carries me bridal style toward the bathroom. I breathe in the scent of his new body wash, the one that smells like sweet rillin. He changed just for me. I kiss his chest and the lights turn up as he sets me on the counter. There are more human things here now because space hasn't fully evolved past the more mundane parts of existence.

We still brush our teeth, I still get the occasional zit, and he still moisturises his gills so they don't chafe. I like it though. There is a vulnerability to having to maintain our bodies together. I like seeing all these parts of us mesh together.

I also like watching my mate bend over.

There is so much back muscularity to watch that it's easy to get lost in him. They shift and flex as he grabs hold of the side to stay out of the stream of water. Ma'xon is well packed, and all that hard muscle he's got is safely protected with the perfect amount of cushion for me.

His tail is thick too. Though I'd never expected to have a thing for it before, how sexy his tail is pops into my head on the regular now. Like how hot I find the girth and length of his tail or how I want to lick the top fin from base to tip like I would his dick.

Is it weird that I've checked out other Axilarian's tails? Probably, but it's mostly out of a desire to know if they are all the same. They aren't. Like people, they come in all sorts of shapes and sizes.

Ma'xon's is the best.

And according to Pri'za, who got a little drunk at our first family dinner all together, you can tell a lot about someone's bedroom prowess based on their tail. So I assume like feet size, it means nothing. I just know I'm hot for my mate's tail and seeing him lose control of it when he comes is one of my favourite things.

I'm so lost in my tail fantasy, I miss him walking over to me. He tucks a finger under my chin until I'm looking up at him. Heat rushes to my cheeks.

"Is this a hot flash?" he asks with complete seriousness.

"No." I smirk. "Just fantasising."

"About what?"

If I've learned anything about Ma'xon, it's that he makes dreams come true. Not even just for me. My mate is a giver through and through. If there is something his people want and dream about, he does whatever he can to make it happen. Which I suppose is why, despite telling me he's retired, he still meets with his local business bureau people for 'meetings', which I think is just code to play golf or the Axilarian version of that.

"About you." I smile, but when I move to jump off the counter a waterfall sensation goes through me and I want to die. "I'm gonna save this for after my period, so expect a business call from me."

"Sex is business for you, pup?" He steps back just enough to grab the edge of my shirt to peel it off me. The air on my skin feels like heaven. Maybe I *am* having a hot flash.

"Oh, super serious, Daddy. One of us will have to take minutes," I tease. This is a dumb conversation to be having with blood dripping down my thigh, but I'm not thinking about my cramps right now and that's what matters.

And more importantly, I like being silly with Ma'xon. I like being able to play and him still finding me sexy and smart and shit. It's been oddly freeing, allowing myself to just speak and not think too hard about it.

"Should I clear my schedule? Plan a breakout session after the meeting? Order catering?" He keeps undressing me but I am now fully distracted by the idea of filling the void inside me with spicy noodles.

"Oh," I draw out. "Let's get dinner from that noodle bar place."

He kisses me, hands swallowing either side of my face like I've got blinders on. There isn't anything else I'd rather see in my view than my shark daddy. Feeling surrounded by Ma'xon until we are meshed together completely is all I want.

While I have never been to a spa before being abducted, the vibes at the dry spa are exactly like what movies show. It's all very serene and there is one of those rock gardens in the foyer. The attendant at the door is calm and polite, with shining rings hanging from her pierced dorsal fin. Ma'xon hands me his card with a kiss on the top of my head before he dashes out for his meeting.

Guess I will be treating myself all alone then. Really, it's much more fun to do this sort of luxury activity, or any activity, with him. Spending his money isn't the kind of spoiling I crave. I want to be spoiled with his intentions, his actions. Handing me a debit card and running away is not it.

At the front desk is a screen that shows off all the services, and it's overwhelming. There are things I understand, like a back massage, but then there are things like a full body excretion that sounds too gross to be real.

"What do you recommend? I need to fill most of the day." I look up at the attendant and her eyes sparkle.

"Have you ever been to a dry spa?" I shake my head at her. "Then you're about to see Sur'lax."

She books me into a full body service. Unlike earth spas, which I always think of as being steam filled and laden with moisturising cream. Dry spas on Axilaria are filled with scrubs and massages that remove all that excess humidity and build-up in the body after being on this planet for any amount of time. Of the few people I see between services, they are mostly humans with a couple of aliens I haven't seen before.

After the facial, I lose track of what's happening around me. I float from one treatment to the next, drinking glasses of water as they're passed to me. Maybe I will see Sur'lax, or God, whoever is real. At this point, someone could ask me for my right arm and I would say 'sure thing!' My eyes are droopy and I have to fight the urge to fall asleep standing up as I'm guided to the sauna.

"You are free to stay here until you're ready to leave the spa. There are refreshments inside, and complimentary toiletries for you to shower afterwards."

My skin is dry without a droplet of sweat and yet I melt into the wooden lounge at the back of the sauna. I've only got a pair of period panties on, but I don't even care. Any concerns about modesty went out the door after the number of naked bodies I've seen today. Nobody gives a shit, and it's great. I summon the strength to sit up when I can no longer resist the pull of dried fruit and nuts. I also down another glass of water because hydration is very important to everyone here.

Through the heat mirage, the sauna doors open and a couple of older humans walk in. They snag handfuls of trail mix and glasses of water before plopping down near me.

"You're Mr. Ma'xon's mate," the man announces, stretching his hand out for me to take.

"Uh-huh." I think I shake it like my dad taught me to, but my energy is completely sapped.

"Settle somethin' for us," the lady next to me says. "Is he retired?"

"He's supposed to be," I grumble. I miss him. What happened to spending the next twenty-five years of our life just being together? My lips turn down in a harsh frown as tears threaten to form.

"Yikes," the man winces before changing the subject. "I'm Lawrence, and this is Betty, by the way. We both moved here at about the same time."

"Odette," I respond, swallowing up my hormones the best I can. "So are you both mated to Axilarians or…?"

"Axilarians," they say at the same time.

I blink away the remaining water in my eyes and I see that both of them have a bite mark similar to mine. Around their shoulders there is just a line of skin that's more shiny and dips around their bicep.

"Er'dex and I met at a happening in the Bronx, 1967. I thought I was on the worst trip of my life," Betty laughs. "We were both young and stupid. They can still be stupid sometimes, but I love them."

"Lor'fe stole my heart over an espresso," Lawrence sighs wistfully, placing a hand on his chest. "I was on my gap year in Sorrento, Italy before I was supposed to be attending uni in London. Most beautiful woman I had ever seen."

"So you've both been here for over fifty years?" I stare at the pair, neither of whom look a day over fifty themselves. "What do you do with your time?"

"I teach swimming, sometimes I volunteer at the local elementary school during their Earth unit," Betty says, leaning back in her lounge chair.

"Lor'fe is a senator, so I spend a lot of time away from the colony doing silly politics now, but since the widespread use of the internet, I mostly just write fanfiction in my free time."

"Ugh, don't get me started on that last thing you sent me."

"It wasn't *that* bad." Lawrence stuffs a date like fruit into his mouth. "You just don't like omegaverse."

"I like omegaverse." I perk up. "Can we get earth books here? 'Cause I have a list of 'em you have to read."

"Hold all of these thoughts, before we leave I need your comm reg," he says.

"Oh, fuck yeah." Betty sits up a bit. "Always happy to have another spa buddy."

They want my communication register, aka my phone number, and I suddenly realise that I have made zero effort to make friends since moving here. I can't even blame it on the obscene amount of sex Ma'xon and I have. When he's not around to go into town, I just lounge by the pool like the housewife I dreamed of being. This is good. I need to make friends other than my mate and being spa buddies sounds great. Real house spouses of Axilaria, here we come!

Until a donut monster bursts into the dry sauna.

I scream. It's only me screaming and then Lawrence and Betty cackling. My warm skin practically explodes with embarrassment when I see Pri'za standing just inside the sauna. She's wearing some life vest with a pool ring float around her gills. No one working here was wearing that, so why is she?

"Are you all done?" she asks.

She crosses her arms, making the ring material squeak, and we burst into laughter. I think she mutters something about the heat going to our heads, but I'm not sure because Lawrence snorts and Betty starts wheezing. It's all so infectious and stupid. Like when the teacher is trying to tell off the class, but it only gets funnier the longer they stand there. It only stops when we are all grabbing our bellies and gasping for air.

"Have you seen Ma'xon today?"

"Not since he dropped me off this morning," I answer, swiping a tear from my eye. "He had a meeting."

A little growl comes out of Pri'za as she pinches the front base of her dorsal fin. So these meetings he's going to are really for work *work* and not just old man networking. My dad used to do a lot of that after he retired, going from Denny's to the golf course to the Moose Lodge. I know my mate isn't doing anything to avoid me because I have eyes. And I see the way he looks at me when he thinks I'm distracted. Plus, anyone within a mile of him can see how the stress weighs on him.

But like all old men, Ma'xon is a stubborn goat.

So rather than admit to his people he doesn't want to talk about bird migrations through the colony or the new senate tax on tourism, he just stands there and listens.

And listens. And listens. Before finally, he says something noncommittal.

Maybe his inaction has gotten him in trouble finally.

"You need to complain more," his sister says. "Because everywhere I turn, someone splashes some new promise he's made to them at me."

"I tried talkin' to him about it." I shrug, thinking about how sideways our conversation went a week ago. It was after the first time we went out to dinner. Every other person there thought they needed to speak to him about colony business. I had eaten my three course meal before he'd even tucked into his appetiser. He didn't have the hearts to tell them to buzz off and when I asked him about it. "He said this was all part of the transition of power, listening to people's problems isn't hurting anyone."

"Uh-huh, well, it's hurting my authority. And it's obviously hurting you."

Out of the corner of my eye, I see Betty reach for the trail mix dish. She and Lawrence are watching us like we're about to have a soap opera level blow out. If Pri'za is fine airing all our laundry out in front of them, so am I.

"Is it that obvious?"

"You look like a neglected pet when his attention is anywhere but on you." Through the heat mirage, her features soften as she sighs. "Which means he is being a very poor mate. And I can't apologise for his errors, but know that when he files for a formal proceedings for these transgressions, I will make sure each step is met with his best."

I blink and look at my spa buddies for clarity.

"Three steps, very bureaucratic, absolutely hilarious," Lawrence whispers.

"I don't need an apology, I just want to spend time with him. He said twenty-five years, not twenty-five minutes."

"Just have him submit his abdication forms again," Betty suggests around a mouthful of nuts.

"But he's already transferred power to me."

"Yes, but there was no ceremony." She lounges back again, throwing one leg over the other. "He just sorta left one day, and we all know people here like a formal shindig."

Lawrence and Pri'za both nod. Clearly, my mate wasn't thinking of the full ramification of his leaving to find a human mate. Which on one hand, when you're burnout like he clearly was, it makes sense. He needed to go, so he did.

"Why not just throw him a retirement party?" I suggest. "That's what happens on Earth. When the newscaster for the radio retired two summers ago, we threw a big ole barbecue for him and everything. The whole town turned up."

"Oh yeah, my dad got a clock when he retired." Lawrence shrugs, but doesn't offer anything more.

"Okay," I say. "But I know Ma'xon doesn't like parties. It's something we matched with on our quizzes. So how are you going to convince him to go?"

"Then we'll make it a surprise party. I can whip something together in a few days. We just have to keep him distracted. Convince him to take you on holiday or something." Pri'za looks downright set on this plan happening now. How is she going to pull this off so quickly?

"Or go back to Earth," Lawrence says.

"What?" That's not an option, right? Is he saying I could have gone back to get my stuff this whole time?

"Lor'fe always says you have the best ideas. That would give us just enough time to set up and spread the word around. I'll call the programme and get it organised for his bounce trip. Odette." Pri'za looks at me. "Think of something back home you have to have, tell him you need it, and Ma'xon will bend over backwards to get it for you."

Betty and Lawrence keep talking about how they can help with the party. The three of them organised a full battle plan in under thirty minutes while I'm just sitting here thinking about all the stuff I left on Earth. Where is it now? Is it safe?

I should just ask Ma'xon.

"Welp." I slap my hands on my knees and stand. "I better go, practitioner has something for me and I'm turning into a raisin."

I make my Midwestern goodbye and speed walk my way to the changing rooms, completely ignoring everyone around me. There is no way I want to go back to Earth. My skin crawls just thinking about possibly running into people I know. It's insane because I left without my say so and I've only been gone a month, but Axilaria is my home. Ma'xon is my home. And no matter how much I think about all my stuff on Earth while I shower, I can't stand the idea of asking him to go all the way back to get it.

"You know," Pri'za says, nearly scaring the bejesus out of me when I step out of the shower. Her silly outfit is off and she's back in her formal colony boss bitch clothes. I scrub my finger against my nose piercing. "It wasn't a surprise to any of us that Ma'xon decided to join the programme. We just never expected him to quit his job too."

I look at her, not exactly sure where she is going with this. Instead, I focus on pulling my own clothes on. One foot in my leggings, then the next before I shimmy them up to my waist.

"I don't think he'd been wholly honest when he told me I'd be taking over. This role can age a person, beyond the physical, and you see what he's like."

"A giver," I murmur.

"He cares too much and let's be real"—she sits down on the bench near my locker—"the colony takes advantage of that."

"Oh that they do," I chuckle. "When he is in that zone, it's almost impossible to get him out of it."

"Which is why we need to push others to come to me or the colony council with their problems," she insists. "So what's with your hesitation?"

"I just—What if he gets upset or feels like we're pushing him?"

"Ma'xon has never been able to do what's good for himself. You are the first thing he has ever done that benefits only him."

My throat closes up. Maybe this isn't what she means, but it sounds like he's trying to give up his throne for me. Like some kind of prince who decided he wanted to wed the milk maid instead of a princess.

I want to be good for Ma'xon, and I want what is best for him even if it sounds as ridiculous as a surprise retirement party.

What harm can a party do anyway?

Chapter 12

Ma'xon

ODETTE STARES AT THE small pod between us. It's bulbous and filled with purple goo that will end her period an hour after she takes it.

If she takes it.

At the practitioner's, she seemed all for a pill that could end her menstrual cycle in an hour. Even the part about it causing bursts of cramps and the sped up evacuation of her uterine lining. An hour of discomfort is better than seven days of bleeding or altering her body's hormone levels.

That is until we got home and she saw what the pill actually was.

"Look, I know a laundry pod when I see one. I am not doing it."

"Pup, that is not what this is."

"I thought it was a pill!"

"It's a gel capsule. I have the same thing in the bathroom for pain relief. All you have to do is bite down on it then swallow the whole thing." I try to sound assuring but her face tells me I am not selling this.

It has not been a great day for me. Knowing my mate was being treated with special luxuries was the only thing that got me through that endless Tails for Axilaria meeting. I hated those when I was in charge, and I still hate them. It's a bunch over centenarians complaining about anything they can from planning permissions to the youth. Nothing pleases them.

All I craved when I met Odette this afternoon was relieving her of her pain as quickly as possible, and then snuggling until we fell asleep. That plan is swimming away faster and faster.

"No." She crosses her arm. "You can't make me, Daddy."

There is something about that little pout on her bottom lip that set me off. Like a tell in a game of chance, I recognise this is a bit of our dynamic. Odette is being a brat on purpose. Whether it's because of something else that happened today or because she has reached her limits with me I don't know. But I will find out.

"I can't?"

She huffs and turns in her stool at the counter. Almost imperceptible, she glances from me to the pod. Maybe leaning into this moment is what I need to relax. There isn't much the Terrainne Rehoming Programme misses.

I know how these relationships can work and how punishment can help both of us.

I take a deep breath. There is a tinge of blood, but there is a touch of her arousal mixed with it. But I want more explicit consent from her.

"Pup, if you don't take the capsule I'll have to punish you." I set my elbows on the counter and look at my little human. "Do you want me to spank you?"

She doesn't even spare me a glance, but the red in her cheeks tells me a lot. "Pssh."

The first time I learned about human's enjoying being smacked on their backside, it was all very technical with zones and anatomy charts. The second time was from a successful couple who volunteered to do a demonstration. While the human partner for that lesson had a dark skin tone, we all watched how his mate checked in with him when a sound he made differed from the others. Like with consent, body language is not always clear.

I don't know if Odette has ever been spanked and I will be putting all my knowledge on the matter to work.

"Trousers off," I command as I stalk around the kitchen toward the couch. "Now."

She blinks at me for a moment before jumping eagerly into action. Her belt is flung across the room and I give her a look as I sit down. If I had an eyebrow I would be raising it, but she chooses to sass me by sticking her tongue out.

She peels her trousers off and my cocks begin to thicken at the sight of her lush thighs.

Odette is beautiful. More beautiful than any flower in the system. More beautiful than the seas and stars combined.

I grab her hips as she nears me, watching how my fingers squish into her body. She's so soft, and all mine.

"Are you going to bore me to death too?"

My jaw drops. When I look at her, there is a smirk on her face.

"Over my knees." I move her as I make the demand. Her hands wrap around my calf and her panty covered ass is in the air. "Two for warm up, six for the attitude."

Odette throws me a thumbs up when I take a fist full of her ass. Good, she's heard me and now we can try spanking for real. With one arm securing her waist, I grip and jiggle each of her cheeks to help warm the skin up. I'm not trying to shock her. I don't want to hurt her.

The first ripple of her bottom when my hand softly collides with her skin is downright addictive though. The little moan she makes when I give the other cheek the same warm up smack makes my hearts thump harder in my chest.

"Doesn't even"—she pushes herself up to look at me over her shoulder—"hurt."

My body lights up when I see her smile. I didn't know I needed that. But now that I have it, I let the power of being her Daddy take control.

My palm cracks against her left ass cheek. Her body jerks, tiny fingernails digging into my skin as she kicks her feet. I wait a beat and then spank her right cheek with the same force.

"Fuck me," she groans.

"Only good pups get to take Daddy's cocks."

I perform the same two smacks again, moving my hands just enough to avoid hitting the same spot, but staying in the safe zone where there is enough muscle and fat to cover anything delicate. This sting should be gone before we even go to bed. This is about allowing us to release tension and roleplay.

She whimpers and I rub my hand over the backs of her thighs.

"Are you sorry for being a brat?" I ask.

"No." She throws that denial up as a green light for the last two spanks.

I inhale, smelling her arousal as my cocks twitch against her hips. There is a tension missing from my shoulders now. Despite the spur of the moment nature of this, I feel better knowing my role and exercising the power Odette gives me.

The last two spanks are a bit harsher and without the wait in between. My pup yelps and when I pull her full up into my lap, she's got tears in her eyes. In unison, we wrap ourselves around each other. She sniffles while I gently rub her back until she is ready to talk.

"Thank you, Daddy." She kisses my chest before looking up at me. "Sorry for springing that on you."

"How do you feel?"

"Kinda light headed from being upside down, but better," she says. "I hope you feel a bit better too."

"I do," I agree. The urge to explain why makes my cheeks warm. "It's nice to have a job and be able to fulfil the role."

"Uh-huh, and is that why you aren't letting Pri'za take your silly meetings?"

I fall back onto the couch and take my mate with me. She giggles and the sound is musical perfection. Her hands press into my torso when she wiggles herself around into a more comfortable position. One that lands her squarely on my hard cocks.

"I can be more needy if you want an excuse to say no to meetings," she continues. "I want you to be happy and not so stressed out. That's not what retirement is about."

"The colony doesn't seem to understand that."

"And you've told them?" She pokes her finger on my snout and I lick her hand in retaliation. I shrug my shoulders because maybe I haven't in so many words made it clear to everyone that my return home doesn't also mean I am returning to my post as colony leader. "You are my Daddy, not theirs. They've got Pri'za to take care of them."

"And as your Daddy, I think it's time for you to take that pill," I say.

"Fine, I'll do your Tide pod challenge, but can I ask a question first?"

"Always, pup."

"You want to spend time with me, right?"

My hearts stop. Odette's voice carries so much vulnerability when she asks me that. I could spend every moment of the rest of my life with her and still it wouldn't be enough time with my mate. I ache to be near her when my big dumb mouth agrees to a meeting. Drowning her with my attention should be my only job, and I'm still failing.

"More than anything," I promise, kissing her softly. "This transition is just taking a bit to set in."

"Some pills are hard to swallow, but we've all got to do it at some point," she says before climbing off me.

I watch her, the bounce in her step that makes her pink backside jiggle hypnotising me. There is nothing I wouldn't do for her. I'd travel to the edge of the known universe if she asked. Axilarians *know* their mates and our bonds are life long. We are a species who have always believed in finding our true mate and giving them our everything.

Why am I not giving Odette the time she wants then? The time that I want for that matter? Did existing in that gooey human body for an evening scramble my brain? I'm filled with questions as I watch my mate pick up the hard pill she's got to take for the better.

She pops the capsule and her eyes widen as she swallows the pod.

"Tastes like a pornstar."

Chapter 13

Odette

Another cramp hits me hard as I slap my comm down on the bathroom counter. They weren't fucking joking about this period ender. My head is a bit heavy, the big caveat to this capsule was that it makes you feel a bit drunk.

"Motherfucker," I grunt and press hard on my lower stomach just as another piece of something falls into the toilet.

My stomach heaves. This last cramp wasn't nearly as bad and Ma'xon has been updating me through the door every fifteen minutes. I've only got another ten or so before I'm done. My legs might be numb from sitting on the toilet for so long, but my fingers worked fine to shoot off a text to Pri'za.

> Me: Booji tep

> Pri'za: Is this one of those drunk human messages lol

> Me: No

> Me: maybbbb

> Me: do the thing

> Pri'za: so bossy >:)

I take a deep breath through my nose and then breathe out my mouth. Another cramp rolls through my uterus, but the pain doesn't radiate or stay long. Nor does anything come out of my body. Praise be. This shit better be like waxing, the more I do it the easier it gets.

·❤·❤·❤·❤·❤·

I wake up clutching the sad pillow again, but when I peel my eyes open, Ma'xon is in bed still. This is the first time this has happened since I told Pri'za we are doing the surprise retirement party. We had to wait another week to get the right provisions from the Solarium Union for Ma'xon to travel back to Earth, but we have it finally.

This is my chance. Now, I just have to ask Ma'xon to get Marbles. Well, assuming the house is untouched, but even a new teddy bear would be vastly better than my current blob.

Which he's glaring at. Perfect.

I shimmy myself across the waterbed until we are almost touching noses. His eyes move back to me and I feel that cosy flutter. The one that fills me with giddiness and hope. Nothing could ever make me regret agreeing to be his. Being abducted is the best dang thing to ever happen to me.

He takes the pillow from my arms and tosses it over his shoulder. He then takes the arm I'm not laying on and drapes it around his neck while he wraps himself around me. Inadvertently, this does shove my other hand right into his gills. His cocks poke at my shins.

"Mornin'." I smile, scratching my fingers around the base of his fin.

"Gimme a reason to stay in bed," he grumbles.

"I mean.." My fingers between his gills wiggle enough to make him jolt. One of his cocks slips between my legs and I tense my calves to tease him more. "It seems like there is plenty a reason to stay with your mate."

Before I can tickle him more, Ma'xon drags me up his body. Angled with my back against the headboard, he yanks my sleep short off. I have just enough time to grab his fin as he licks me from bottom to top. My eyes flutter shut as I let the feeling wash over me. His tongue, his head between my thighs, his hand squeezing my butt cheek—the perfect way to wake up.

He nuzzles into my pussy, burying his tongue inside me. I whimper and grind my clit against his nose, trying to send the message of where I want his attention. But he's never been one for body language.

"More," I moan, thrusting uselessly against him. "Daddy, more."

"Mmm," he rumbles against me with a beautiful vibration that makes me clench, but then he pulls away. "Still feeling bratty?"

My body tingles when he says the word. Turns out complaining more and being a naughty pup really does get results. It didn't completely fix our situation, but playing up my attitude has gotten him to cancel a couple more meetings. I'll do whatever it takes to get him to relax.

Plus, it's fun.

"Yes, now I want to come."

You can mark this new behaviour as impossible as being abducted by aliens. Until last week, I would have sworn against being a brat. I never thought I had it in me to be anything but sweet when it came to our dynamic. Turns out, I really like pushing Ma'xon's buttons until he bends me over his knee.

Or puts me on mine.

I'm lifted again, squeaking as we jostle around until I see my sad blob pillow on the floor.

"Hey," I whine.

"Let's put this to good use while we get your attitude adjusted, pup."

He sets me down between his spread thighs and both of his cocks are there for the taking. All mine. I can taste the salted caramel flavour of his cum already.

My knees sink into the pillow and my fingers into his thighs. Asking him to go to Earth can wait. Dick sucking can't.

"How are you feeling?" he asks.

Every time Ma'xon checks in with me, I feel a little bit more cherished. He takes my chin between his fingers to tear my gaze from his cocks. His thumb pulls on my bottom lip and I have to lick it.

Teasing is always good.

"Hungry for cock, Daddy."

His cheeks darken to that adorable navy colour, but his eyes show just how hungry he is too. God, I love this shark man.

"Open your mouth."

He takes his bottom shaft in hand, stroking it until his frills are exposed and glistening with lilac precum. I do as he says, tongue on my lower lip while I wait for the green light.

Ma'xon also likes to tease me when I'm being a brat.

His frills tickle when he taps the head of his cock against my tongue. I taste the saltiness and try to lick up what I can without closing my mouth. My clit throbs the longer I'm forced to kneel and watch.

Finally, achingly slowly, he leans into me enough to feed the head of his dick into my mouth. My lips stretch wide as he holds there, letting me adjust to his frills. I swallow once and I'm ready for more. The flavour of Ma'xon on my tongue is my driving force.

His top cock dribbles precum down my cheek as I carefully start to suck. I have learned the hard way not to be too enthusiastic at the start. The last thing I want is another frill in my eye.

"There ya go, pup," he praises me. "Keep sucking on Daddy's cock."

When he calls himself Daddy, I wanna cream my non-existent jeans. Every time. It makes my pussy clench with need. There is something so undeniably sexy about the way he says the word, the way he claims the title. I take more of him into my mouth but it's only just past the head. My breathing is measured through my nose as I try to lose myself in this.

I can't stop squirming though. Something is missing. I double tap his thigh. Instantly my mouth is cock free and I take a big gulp of air.

"Do you need a break or another pillow?"

I assess where I'm at comfort wise and shake my head. That part is all fine and dandy. What I want is to lose a bit of control.

"Can you push my head?"

"'Course pup, thank you for asking." He smiles at me and my insides threaten to burst with joy. This is what I need in a relationship. He is understanding and respectful of what I like. He knows my boundaries and waits for me to hand over those tiny little nuggets of control, rather than taking my kink gold mine for himself.

His hand comes up to my cheek first, caressing me before his fingers weave into my hair. I open my mouth and wait for him to guide me. *Yes, lead me Daddy, show me who's boss.*

The pressure is gentle and sweet. Ma'xon doesn't take his eyes off me as he starts to use my mouth. He moves me in short, shallow thrusts. His hips meet me in the middle, so his hand holds me in place. More of his cock shoves into my mouth and it hits the back of my throat.

He moans and my eyes close. There it is, the missing piece that kept me from slipping into this moment. We're connected now. Even as he uses my mouth for his pleasure, I feel special and cared for. He's still holding me as I drool over his cock and my chin.

"So precious for me. My good little pup when you get what you need." He groans when I hum in agreement. The frills in the back of my throat make me gag, but Ma'xon doesn't stop. "Get ready to swallow."

My fingers squeeze his thighs tighter as his body tenses. Ma'xon pulls me back until just the tip is in my mouth. I keep my eyes closed. Ready for a double whammy.

His frills spasm and ropes of cum coat my tongue. I swallow as much as I can, moaning at how sweet it is. His tail slaps against the mattress as he grunts.

My face is dry.

His softening, messy cock slips from my lips and when I look up, I see his fist locked around the other one, still hard and frills exposed.

"What're?" I swallow the last half of my question, feeling the effect of less oxygen and the high of sex.

"We aren't done yet."

A grin, giddy and wicked, spreads across my face. I'm ready to put the sass away, but if Ma'xon still wants to play I am so game.

"Just one dick?" I sigh like it's a let down, like it's not a feat that I'm able to take one. "Not sure what that'll do."

"Pup, I think you're getting too big for your space pants."

He pulls me up gently by the hand in my hair to capture me in a devastating kiss. His tongue plunges into my mouth and I swear I taste green apples. My hands shake in their position on his thighs. I really need to ask more questions about Axilarian anatomy because right now I have no idea if this is all in my head or if Ma'xon is going to have another mating frenzy.

Not that he gives me much time for educational questions. He pulls us back up onto the bed and spins me around enough that I feel like cotton candy at the county fair. Sweet, fluffy, and ready to melt in his mouth. My shirts come off and he puts my hands on the headboard.

"Keep them here, pup," he says with a squeeze. His whole body cages me in, hands bracketing mine, his knees on either side of my hips, and his hard cock pulsing against my wet pussy. "Daddy's going to fuck that attitude right out of you."

"Oh shit," I whimper.

"I want to hear you sing for me."

His hips pull back. My body buzzes and tingles with so much anticipation I think I might cry. Everything about this is so fucking hot. His weight on me, that goddamn Daddy voice he does, the thrill that I am the one he is this desperate for; it's a cocktail of emotions that is screaming at me to beg and shout.

"Daddy…" I say when he kisses my neck. My head easily falls to the side, ready to feel his teeth, craving his bite.

"What does a good pup say?"

"Please fuck me, Daddy, I won't be a brat again," I promise.

He thrusts. His cock fills me to the brim and I still want more, until I'm spilling over with him. My elbows shake with the power of him. The bottom cock is half hard and rubs over me. As he pulls back, it drags against my neglected clit until my hips are rolling, trying to fuck myself into Ma'xon. He smiles against my throat.

"Love you, Odette, until the seas wash me away, I will always love you."

Tears slip down my cheeks. He drives into me again and I shout with pleasure. I am full and my body feels like it's a million degrees. The stretch is delicious. This is perfect. Exactly where I am meant to be.

"Yes," I scream. "Ma'xon, faster, please."

His hands move over mine as my world shakes. Over and over, he slams into me. Our bodies clap and cheer every time he bottoms out. His second dick is hard, the frills exposed and taunting my clit now. Inside of me, his cock is smooth and slick. He glides in and out, in and out, like we are made for one another.

Sweat slicks my back while tears dribble down my cheeks. I can't form a coherent thought. I don't know which way is up, I just know that if I keep pushing back into the cradle of Ma'xon's hips, his cock touches that spot so deep inside of me I see galaxies behind my eyes.

"Daddy, fuckin' me so good," I moan. "Gonna come."

"Sur'lax, yes, give it to me, pup. Make a mess on this cock. S'all yours."

His hands flex around mine when he says it's all mine. I know we are mated for life. He is mine, my daddy. But it sends me over my edge when he says it out loud. My pussy spasms around his cock, clenching hard enough that the rest of me shakes with the tension.

I sing for him just like he asked.

Chapter 14

Ma'xon

Something is going on under my fins. I can feel it in the tips of my tail. Not because of anything that happened this morning, more so what's been going on this week. Odette has been hyper aware of her comm, always acting chipper to see me leave. But she has also been bratty and very demanding when she wants attention. That attitude appeals to me more and more every time she brings it out.

Also it's not quantum science. I have eyes. The bags in the pool shed are filled with craft supplies for something.

Once Odette has gotten fed up with being sticky, we shower and make breakfast. Another reason this sassy attitude of hers is growing on me is how sweet she is after. Like she is trying to apologise to me for something I am wholeheartedly behind. We sit at the counter, with me on a stool and her in front of me like the most delicious meal she is.

"Are you sure?" she asks.

"Promise, cross my tail fin," I answer, leaning in to hug her more.

"Okay, I still think we need a signal for when we wanna be extra. Ya know, like a tie on the door or something."

"Why don't you make a sign?" I suggest, covertly asking if that's what the art stuff is for. "Like brat in session."

"Maybe, but crafts aren't really my thing."

She grabs a piece of fruit and feeds it to me. I suck the sweet juice off her fingers and she giggles when I try to nibble at them. There's a flush in her cheeks when she grins at me, but then it fades as she bites her bottom lip. Her eyebrows bunch together in a way that makes me want to kiss away her worries. What's this all about?

"Can I ask you something?"

"Always, pup."

"You know sad blob pillow?"

The bane of my existence as a mate? Of course, I know exactly what object she is talking about. We spent a whole day going through every home store and thrift shop in the colony trying to find anything that resembles this elusive teddy bear that my pup misses from Earth.

It's not uncommon for the non-human half of TRP pairings to put their mate into the pod and then scour their homes for items of comfort to help them adjust to their new life. It's usually simple things, maybe just a backpack or a small heirloom from a relative.

But I was in too much of a rush. She even invited me to her home. I could have seen what Odette's life was like, but I'm a complete x'rox who was too selfish. It wouldn't have killed me to go home with her. I could have driven us back to my ship in her small earth vehicle with that stuffed bear strapped in with her.

"I was wondering if it was possible to go back to Earth?" she asks in a rush. "Just to get Marbles from my house. I don't want to stay and it would be super quick, in and out, and-and-and—"

"And I will make a call today," I finish for her.

This is the least I can do. I don't know if these sorts of trips happen often or if I will have to pull every connection I have at the senate to get this unplanned trip approved, but I will do whatever it takes.

There is a visible weight lifted off her shoulders. Nothing should burden her like this. It was my first promise to her, to spoil her and take away stress.

Really, it's Odette that does this for me. Every moment with her is like slipping into cool water on a boiling hot day. She's been paddling along and swimming through the tidal wave of insanity I thrust upon her. The world floats when it's just the two of us. We have made our own dream island a real place.

· ❤ · ❤ · ❤ · ❤ · ❤ ·

I get a call from my sister too soon after I call the colony clerk about the form to request clearance to travel to Earth. Between meetings, I see the long form communication that my trip has been pre-approved and I can leave today in a single-being craft. Leaving without Odette isn't ideal, but I will do what I must for my mate. I haven't even finished reading it when Pri'za's avatar dings on my device.

"Why are you going back to Earth?" she demands.

"Why do you use your powers for evil?" I ask.

I should've known when I handed my position of colony leader to Pri'za she would use it to keep tabs on me as well. She likes to know every detail about everyone in the colony. There isn't a secret she can't dig up from the depths.

"Some of us are just better," she says. "Now what's on Earth?"

"Odette needs something."

It will not be my lips she pries the stuffed animal secret out from. When the topic of Marbles first came up, my mate seemed a little embarrassed about needing a plush toy to sleep with. It's not something we have for Axilarian youth, but I know many people who still chew on their favourite fefe toy into their eighties.

Comfort is comfort.

"Fine," she huffs. "Is Odette going with you?"

"I was approved for a one seater."

"She can stay with us if she wants while you're away. Closer to town and the girls have been dying for a sleepover. They don't exactly get that just because they are of similar age, that Odette may not want to play dress up."

I lose track of the conversation for a moment thinking about the last time she did play dress up for me. The very strict instructions I received to observe the fashion show to completion and not try to feel her up every chance I got was maddening. We made it through one outfit before I was dragging her down to the floor to devour her pussy.

"Does she know you're not going to take her?"

I snap back to our call. "No, and don't tell her I am going to earth. I want to surprise her when I return with her things."

There is a beat of silence over the comm and I wonder if my sister has simply hung up on me.

"And how will you explain your absence to your new mate who you already neglect?"

"I do not—"

"Where is she right now?"

Having a second offspring was the worst mistake my parents ever made. My life would be oceans easier as an only child.

"She's at home," I grumble. "You don't have to be right all the time."

"I do. And I won't tell her you're going to earth."

She hangs up on that promise. It's good that she at least approved of my idea to surprise Odette.

The sooner I leave, the sooner I will be back home in her arms. I'm not sure how I will handle going without her touch for more than a few hours. Her laughter won't be in my ears. I check the travel confirmation once more. I can leave as soon as I'm ready, but all I'm ready for is to be back. This meeting doesn't need me here, it's not my job anyway.

On my way home again, I leave a voice note for Pri'za.

"If you want to attend the ToA meeting today, you better get to it now. I'll be back in two days."

·♥·♥·♥·♥·♥·

Odette is baking when I get home. From the stairs, I can smell the warm sweet scent wafting through the air.

She's singing too.

This is the first time I've ever heard it in real life. I know what her career involved back on earth, recording ads and what not for radio broadcasting. But there is something mystical about hearing this unedited version of her. The rise in her voice's pitch, the little wobble when it goes a bit too low for her register. It's hypnotising.

My hearts beat wildly as I climb the stairs two at a time to get to her. The curtain over the door sways gently in the breeze and tangles with my tail. She shrieks when she turns, but quickly dissolves into laughter at my predicament.

"You're home early," she says with a smile, arranging chunky disks on a wire rack.

My thoughts are as twisted as the curtain on me. "What are those?"

"Cookies, I had a craving," she says into the microheater, another tray of sweet disks placed inside.

"You have a beautiful voice."

She turns around quickly, face flushed from something more than baking. Loose hairs frame her shoulders and cheeks. The most beautiful being in the galaxy, in the universe. I'm practically floating when she's within arms reach.

And she reaches out to grab me by the waistband of my trousers. Her softness molds to me and warmth spreads inside me. Her small hand smooths up and down my back as we embrace. I wonder how I'm going to survive without her touch even for such a short period of time?

"I have to leave for an emergency meeting at the senate. Today."

"Is this because you asked to go to Earth?" she asks. "I didn't know it would be so much trouble, you don't have to."

I squeeze her softness, slowly dancing us around to the tune that she was just singing. "It's no trouble."

"How long will you be gone?"

"About two days, assuming everything goes smoothly."

There is a short hesitation before she speaks. I am not sure if she simply didn't hear me or if her thoughts are back to something else.

"I can stay with Pri'za, I suppose."

"Did she call you?" I ask. Her body stiffens a little and I pull back to look at her. "You okay?"

"Yeah, yeah," she swallows. "Uh, no she didn't call me, but I'm sure she wouldn't mind getting lunch or something, ya know? Girl time."

I hum, leaning down until we are eye level. A little, nervous laugh comes out of my mate. Odette's eyes are as beautiful as the rest of her, yet I know they hold something deeper. The supplies in the pool shed, the immediacy of my trip to earth, something is being planned behind my back and I don't like it.

Maybe I am just as nosey as my sister.

Odette squirms under my attention. When the microheater rings, her eyes flick toward the machine and I know I've got her cornered. She can't look me in the eye again and if it weren't so adorable I'd probably be a little annoyed.

"You can't tell Pri'za I spilled the beans," she whispers. "It's a surprise."

A grin that is way too smug spreads across my face. My tail swishes back and forth with delight at getting her to tell me. So they are trying to send me away for a short time on purpose. That explains how easy it was for me to get a return trip to Earth, but I'm not sure why I can't know about what they are planning.

"What's the surprise?" I ask.

"Nope, nuh-uh, I have to keep some secrets." She twists around so she can't see me anymore. She folds her arms across chest as if she is closing our conversation. But I am just as bad as my sister. I want to know everything, especially if we are surprising someone.

"Do you though?" I tickle her soft sides

"Ma'xon," she gasps. "Yes, now go do the things so you can come back to me sooner."

When I lift Odette up and spin her around, she laughs and laughs, and my hearts fill with so much happiness I forget about my own surprise for her. I put her down on the counter just to look in her eyes again without bending so much. She is filled with joy, and therefore so am I.

Odette winds her arms around me and all I can think is this is my life. I can't ask for anything more. This is why I have to do this for her, why I am desperate to bring her teddy bear back from Earth much sooner than she believes.

"Will you sing for me when I get back?" I ask.

"Every day we're together," she promises, before stuffing a cookie in my mouth. "Now skedaddle."

·♥·♥·♥·♥·♥·

Letters of resignation are sent to employers, fake trips scheduled with no return, homes emptied, and contents placed in TRP owned storage containers. It's all standard procedure now. The Solarium Union is nothing without their bureaucracy.

It makes this trip to Earth much more comfortable. No one cocked goo bodies or anxiety to worry about.

Well there is some anxiety as I land in this frozen tundra at the southernmost point of Earth. What if I can't find the mysterious Marbles? Returning home empty handed is not an option. I could enquire with the receptionist if there are any units available for purchase and root around in those, but it would take up more time, meaning longer away from my pup.

No, I will find my mate's teddy bear if it's the last thing I do. And it very well could be if I freeze to death. The tips of my fins are numb and my gums ache with how much my teeth chatter as I walk through the polytunnel from the landing bay to the storage facility. It's not even a long walk, but I think of home; the humidity, two suns, and Odette's hot pussy wrapped around my cocks.

I see why some beings evolved to have pockets or sheaths. I would kill for an extra layer of that protection right now. At the door there is an electric keypad and I have to pull up my comm to remember the passcode, but the moment I'm in hot dry air blows down from the door.

Praise Sur'lax.

If that is the hardest part of this journey, I will take it. While I would do most anything for my pup, I am not an Axilarian built for the ice tundra. After the reception gives me an old school keycard, I am on my own to find and swipe what I need from the unit. Again, bureaucracy and order reigns because all I have to do is follow the signs down the well lit halls.

It's almost easy.

Though I am not surprised when I open the bay doors to the unit that I am going to eat my words. Before me, mountains of brown boxes and carefully wrapped shapes stand between me and Marbles. I read each label on the boxes, some are labelled by room, like 'bathroom' or 'kitchen', others are labelled by contents.

"Books, books, blankets, candles. How does she own enough candles for a whole box?"

Perhaps it is rude of me to snoop through my mate's belongings, but this feels almost like an expedition into her mind and her past. I am an explorer of old in search of new planets and life. I stretch my arms and crack my tail before I lift the candle box down from a shelf and onto the floor.

Pulling a muscle or bending cartilage is not on the docket for today.

I open the box and see twenty or more unopened boxes, each of them with different labels and descriptions. There is one that claims to smell like the disks Odette was making before I left and I rip that open. It smells synthetic and nothing at all like her cookies. There are others that smell like forests and dead animal skins and elusive emotions that don't make sense.

There is one with a dark and foiled label that catches my eye. *Boudoir Love Rituals*. I don't know what that b-word is, but if there is a human love ritual that Odette felt so called to she purchased some sort of scent for it, it's coming home with me.

I set it aside and continue to excavate my way through the storage unit. Each time I find an item that could be important, I add it to the growing pile of things I will have to stuff into my single seat pod. Adult pleasure toys in odd shapes, a book on house plants, a small photograph of two adults and a small baby that looks like Odette, and a pair of undergarments that have a slit down the middle. I'm not sure what good the last item I toss onto my small pile is, but they give me ideas.

Ideas of spreading my mate open while she wears them and nothing else. Is that what the ritual candle is also a part of?

I'm working my way through the final box labelled 'bedroom', with my cocks aching in the trousers, when finally I come upon a worn and somewhat small soft toy. Its fur is discoloured. There are clumsy and mismatched stitches covering its arm and neck, and it has black unseeing eyes that I am sure will haunt me for the rest of my days. Still, when I breathe in to sigh with relief, I smell

Odette. Her scent clings to this plush in a way that is oddly comforting.

"Marbles, you better be good to my pup."

I grab a bag hanging from the wall quickly and stuff my findings inside before tucking the teddy bear under my arms. It's time to get home to my mate.

Chapter 15

ODETTE

OH NO.

Oh no no no no.

This is a disaster. The exact opposite of how this surprise party is supposed to get set up. Ma'xon will be here any moment. He's called to say he is only a tick away. That's barely thirty minutes, that's not enough time and yet it isn't soon enough. Every part of me wants to wrap myself around Ma'xon like a big boa constrictor and never let go, but we need more time.

The catering was over an hour late, so all the food is still uncooked. They are hard at work setting up hibachi style grills, but that means the only nibbles we have set up are billions of cookies I stress baked to fill the void of Ma'xon being away.

And cookies, despite how delicious they are, can't really fill voids like noodles can.

The banner Ke'lee and A'la made refuses to stay attached to the wall across from the entrance to colony hall. If I put any more of that sticky gunk Lawrence gave me up there it's gonna ruin the paint, or whatever the coating is.

And let's not forget the fact that I am desperately trying to keep this outfit clean.

Formal wear in Axilaria is formal. I'm not talking black tie and ball gowns. I'm talking wearing this very specific shade of blue belt skirt with sparkles and this sleeveless jumpsuit with mesh and fancy piping to signify I'm mated to the man of the hour. Everyone is in a varying shade of blue, but I am the only one in this iridescent colour.

The moment Pri'za started to spread the word that there would be a colony wide celebration to honour Ma'xon's years of service, she was inundated with offers to help. Lawrence rescheduled Lor'fe's return to senate so she could hand my mate an official certificate. Betty's mate, Er'dex, apparently owns a flower shop, and they're bringing a full spectrum of blooms to liven up the boring lobby.

I will never be able to express how grateful I am that Pri'za is the one in charge of this planning. As I step off the mag-lift platform, another person walks up to her with an attitude. I've never been one to handle that sort of conflict. One time my boss told me I had to re-record an ad because he didn't like the way I said butter and I just left for my lunch early. The customer had approved the ad, I wasn't going to make any more changes.

Pri'za handles conflict like the leader she clearly is. It's not that she takes everything people say to her in strides the way Ma'xon does, it's that she seems to know whatever someone is going to have a problem with before they even say it. She's like a magician. She's absolutely found what she loves and made it her life. Which is knowing everyone's business and telling them how to make it better.

She's also a little scary.

"Odette," she barks. "Where are we on refreshments?"

"All ready to go," I say with a mock salute. "Signs up, grills are on, and Al'dren has the girls already at the house ready for surprise one."

She does a little hype dance that makes her tail swish back and forth so fast I can't see the tips of it. This party is as much a benefit to Ma'xon as it is to her. She is showing the colony how ready she is to lead, and she is doing it swimmingly.

"This is your final warning," she shouts into her comms, which blasts the message through the intercom system around the hall.

Overkill? Maybe. Totally effective at getting everyone to scramble? Absolutely.

Axilarians start rushing around like a load of chickens with their heads cut off. Everywhere I look, someone is carrying another tray of appetisers around or setting up more makeshift tables with long cloths so we all have space to hide. Every time I complete a task for someone, another person needs an extra hand.

I'm exhausted by the time I finished wrapping the last Ialot garland around the stair railing to block off the first floor of the building. Sweat drips down my back and I have never wished for a fan more in my life.

Pri'za's comm goes off with an alert from Al'dren.

They're almost here.

As predicted people start doing that silly speed walk you do when you're trying to sneak by quickly without getting caught. I don't get why or how this is such a universal thing, even a billion miles from Earth, but that doesn't mean I don't get caught up in the excitement. I'm on my tiptoes just like everyone else and running towards the front entrance. Between dodging someone's tail and stepping over the legs of the tripod for the motion camera, disaster strikes.

One second I am pristine in my formal attire, the next I am covered in green juice that smells too much like beer. There is a resounding gasp around me and people are staring at me. And the flash goes off.

Not only have I ruined my top, there is photographic evidence of it for all to see.

Why does this happen to me? What have I done to upset the universe so much?

In a panic, I grab hold of a corner of a table cloth to wipe my shirt clean and the person whose juice I'm wearing dashes for a closet in the back corner of the room. Pri'za grabs each of my biceps suddenly and lifts. We're moving before I can make a sound. It isn't until we are behind the receptionist desk that she drops me. She shoves away the couple hiding here and turns to me.

"Don't panic," she says.

"I'm totally chill," I lie. She knows I'm lying too because there are tears running down my cheeks and I can't stop my chin from wobbling. "I'm like an ice—ice—"

"There is a lost items box." She pulls it out and I'm staring at the most villainous collection of belongings I've ever seen. And I worked in radio.

Pri'za tosses away a three cupped bra, a crystal dildo that is too realistic, poker chips, a half burnt playbill, and one fingerless glove meant from someone with only two fingers. Finally she pulls at a new top that looks like it's all mesh. Not even a full horizontal strip across the chest for tits or decoration.

Her cheeks turn navy the longer she stares at it.

"Show me." I hold my breath. She turns the top around and I read it aloud. "Frill seeker."

Is this worse than 'Lik This'? At least it's all spelled correctly. I can't form any other thoughts. My inappropriate shirt doesn't have the grammatical errors that horrible shirt I wore on my first date with Ma'xon does. That's all I can think about.

"We'll manipulate the pictures before we share them anywhere," she promises. "I'll try and stall for a few."

She sprints toward the entrance. I hear her loudly greet Ma'xon and my body starts moving. I rip off my formal top and slide into this mesh monstrosity. At least my nipples are covered. I know Axilarian's don't have them, but lord help me. I am not flashing nip on camera.

I peek out over the desk and can just make eye contact with Betty. I make a face and show her my front, pointing down at my chest. Her eyes bug out when she reads it and slaps a hand over her mouth. Her thumb pops up in approval and that's the last chance I get before I hear feet stomping up the stairs.

It's now or never. My stomach is a nervous ball of knots and all I can think about is how much I want to hug Ma'xon. This has been the busiest two days of my life. There hasn't been time to stop and miss my mate. I haven't been able to think of anything but planning and planning and how much I don't want children after staying with Pri'za and Al'dren.

All I want is to snuggle up with my giant shark man and slurp down a bucket of noodles. Maybe also have my back blown out, but that's secondary.

My primary objective is wrapping myself around Ma'xon so he never leaves me again. I spent the first twenty-eight years of my life completely fine with just a teddy bear to give me comfort. But now? Now I need an eight foot tall alien with a tail to hold me close at night and tell me about his favourite flowers or what happened at Ke'lee's last birthday party.

I need the sound of his voice in my ear, telling me how much my laughter makes him smile or how gorgeous he thinks I am dripping wet. Ma'xon has invaded all the spaces around me and I know I've done the same to him.

"SURPRISE!" everyone shouts.

Flower petals shower the entrance and the camera flashes, capturing the awe on Ma'xon's face. I rush around the desk and throw myself at him like they do in the movies when the love interests are reunited after a long time apart.

It's been two days, hardly any time in the grand scheme of my new extended life, yet I burst into tears when we make eye contact. He takes two long strides and then I'm being lifted high into the air. I look down at my mate, my Ma'xon. There he is, all mine.

"Don't ever leave again," I sniffle, wrapping my legs just under his armpits.

"Not without you by my side," he promises.

He winds his arms around me and nuzzles into my shoulder. He presses kisses onto my skin all the while the people around try pushing us along toward the podium so the party can get started. But Ma'xon won't be moved just yet. He pulls away from our hug long enough to press his lips to mine.

I sigh into the kiss. Oh yeah, this is what I may have missed more than cuddling. The taste of him on my lips, on my tongue, it's like everything I didn't know I was missing. Our relationship is still so new, but we fit together like an old married couple. Spending the next twenty five years just being together doesn't seem long enough now.

"Are you done yet?" Pri'za asks.

We aren't. We never will be. But for the sake of everybody's eyeballs, I put a pause on our reunion so we can get this first part of the retirement ceremony done. I want Lor'fe to hand over the certificate, to steal two plates of spicy noodles, and to run back to the house so I can spend the rest of my life enjoying my mate.

But that's very wishful thinking.

Like Betty said, Axilarian's love a good ceremony. Lor'fe stands at the podium behind us, patiently waiting for Pri'za and Ma'xon to come up onto the stage. All around me, Axilarians form neat and quiet rows around the stage and tables. They don't even swish their tails. Ma'xon's fingers linger in mine until we have to part again for him to step up to the podium.

"Today, we celebrate a great Axilarian," Lor'fe starts and oh my god, I'm going to cry. She keeps talking, expressing her gratitude to Ma'xon and all his work to make our colony beautiful and homely, but all my focus is on him.

How his cheeks are tinted navy and how the muscles in his chest flex when he holds his hands behind him.

It's only when Lor'fe steps aside and he takes her space that I see the ratty old tote bag on the ground. Oh, fuck. Where did he find that? Clear as day to everyone in attendance, there is a massive, lewd werewolf illustration on display. I know that bag. When I was in college, I carried that bag around with pride everywhere.

However.

It's not something I necessarily want to be remembered for and already I can see Lawrence trying to sneakily get my attention from across the room. He tilts his head towards the bag and I'm certain if this was a dry planet I would burst into flames with my blush alone. Where on this planet did he get that bag? Was it something I had in my car that he forgot to mention? Ma'xon is still saying his thank yous to everyone and it's only when he says my name that I stop dissociating about my werewolf bag.

"Odette, my mate, I'm sorry I haven't made the time for you I should have been, taking these meetings and prioritising our time as second. This party made me realise that I'm the one who needs to reprioritise. I can't thank you enough for trusting me, for waiting for me to get off my tail. But I have a surprise for you as well." Ma'xon holds out his hand for me as I carefully step up to him. My heart is racing, thundering in my ears so loud I can only focus on my shark man. He bends down and picks up the bag.

"For an Axilarian, a promise is a contract that is as strong as the currents above."

Oh sweet baby Jesus, what is going to come out of that bag?

"I promised to take care of you, give you everything you could ever want, and all you have asked for is me."

Goddamn it all, I'm going to cry again. In front of everyone and their mothers, but I have never felt so loved by another being than right now with Ma'xon looking at me. I don't care what comes out of that bag, it could be space cooties. I don't care because it's coming from someone who cared deeply enough for me to travel all the way back to Earth for it.

"And, of course, Marbles."

Maybe in a few days I will feel embarrassed about this, but when he pulls my teddy bear out, I scream and scramble to wrap my arms around it before I'm wrapping myself around him too. It smells like my old home, like years spent singing into a hairbrush and wishing boys would like me. But I don't want *or* need boys and there is only one being I want to sing to now. Tears stream down my face while I tell him thank you over and over. He scoops up into his arms. God, I love it when he does this.

"I love you," I say, smearing tears across his tank top. "So, so, much. You don't even know."

"We'll just have to show each other, won't we, pup?" he whispers, before kissing me.

·❤·❤·❤·❤·❤·

After shaking a few more hands, all it takes is one look from me with a tiffin tin in one hand and the tote bag slung over my other arm, for Ma'xon to leave. I hear the distinct words, *have a chat with my sister about your concerns*, and my heart swells a little. I know that is a big change for him and that this will take time to adjust, but I already see the people waving at him as they head for Pri'za.

As he approaches, I expect him to take my hand as we sneak out of colony hall, but instead he takes the takeaway from me and lifts me off the ground to cradle me in his side. The werewolf tote with Marbles in it is tucked securely into my elbow.

"You're amazing, ya know that?" he says, looking down at me. There is so much love in his eyes, it's tooth rotting.

"Pssh." I smile, leaning into him. "I missed you."

"I'm never taking a single unit pod for an interplanetary travel again," he starts, keeping up a steady pace as he tells me the details of his trip. Even once we are on the empty tram, he can't seem to stop talking. "And let me tell you, tundra is not as nice as it sounds. How do beings live in those conditions?"

"They wear more clothes," I say with a poke to his bare arm. "So all my stuff is in a lock up? Totally fine?"

"Impressively well packed. I couldn't tell you how they got it all to fit."

I choke, half snorting, half laughing. "They made it fit, Daddy."

It takes a moment to register, and then he looks down at me on his lap with navy cheeks. How could I not say it? The joke was right there in front of me.

"Terrible," he laughs. "And I see you have found more suggestive clothes to wear."

"What? This old thing?" I look down at my mesh shirt. "I ran into someone right before you came in and got juice all over my nice top. This was all that was in lost and found."

"Mmm," he hums, looking me over and then he smiles. "I think I much prefer shirts with instructions."

Once I start laughing, I can't stop. I don't know what it is that is so funny, maybe it's the joy of having my mate back or maybe it's something else, but tears well in my eyes and Ma'xon is there to wipe them away.

He presses his forehead to mine.

I can't believe this is my life.

Epilogue

The Interview

Odette on Ma'xon

What were you hoping for?

To find someone who understands the importance of breakfast.

First impressions after abduction?

Embarrassment mostly, I was worried I'd pee my pants.

Best thing about Ma'xon?

His hearts, how he is so giving and caring and thoughtful of everyone around him.

If you could change one thing about the programme, what would it be?

An intro presentation on what's happened would be handy.

Would you introduce Ma'xon to your friends?

Of course! Well, after they have a chance to adjust to aliens.

Describe Ma'xon in three words.

Kind, Handsome, Sweet

Marks out of 10?

10,000/10

And how would you rate your experience in the Terrainne Rehoming Programme?

A big fat 5 stars

·♥·♥·♥·♥·♥·

Ma'xon on Odette

What were you hoping for?

To find a mate who saw the beauty in my planet.

First impressions after abduction?

Panic and need, I was a mess and she was so relaxed.

Best thing about Odette?

Her laughter, getting to be a part of her joy.

If you could change one thing about the programme, what would it be?

A parcel shipment service post mating.

Would you introduce Odette to your friends?

It fills me with great pride to introduce Odette to all my people as my mate.

Describe Odette in three words.

Funny, warm, generous

Marks out of 10?

10/10, she's perfect

Epilogue

Ma'xon

THE BLACK SAND BEACHES are beautiful this time of year. Not as beautiful as my mate who is attempting to bury me in the hot sand, but nothing really does compare to her. Around us, there are few other vacationers. Axilarians and off-worlders alike flock here year round to enjoy a much deserved break from the humdrum of life.

We are here simply for a change of scenery.

A few months ago, Odette mentioned she'd never seen the ocean on Earth. We've been travelling through all the local beaches since. I'm not going to deprive my mate of suns, bubbly drinks, and risky sex.

Another double fist full of sand is placed over my feet. She hums a choral tune she has been learning with a small group from our colony as she works. There are a few notes she can't hit because she lacks gills, but even as she swallows the sounds I find it a perfect accompaniment to our vacation. Once she is finished, she scrubs her hands clean across the front of her striped swimsuit.

"Don't move, I'm gonna take a picture," she commands.

"Get my good side." I smile and crane my neck a little. It's really the only part of me I can move at this point, but I feel surprisingly relaxed with all this warmth packed in around me.

"1...2...got it!"

Just because I'm relaxed doesn't mean I want to stay buried. I shake my whole body loose, spray sand everywhere while Odette shouts and giggles, running for the warm water. We learned very quickly she hates the feeling of sand getting stuck to her, especially the more delicate places. I follow after her and dive beneath a wave.

Her little feet kick beneath me and I can't resist giving her another tease. I tickle her ankles, narrowly avoiding the well earned kick she lets loose. When I pop up above the surface, she splashes me.

"Look," she says, swimming up to me to wrap her arms and legs around my torso. "If you're gonna act like a shark, we should at least watch *JAWS*."

I kick my feet to keep us in place as the waves slowly roll over us. The heat between her thighs bounces against my chest with the motion and my cocks chub up in my tight trunks. My body aches for her as much as it did when we first mated, more so even as we have grown closer and closer. She finishes my sentences, lets me do mundane and silly tasks for her that fills me with a sense of purpose, she holds me close in her sleep because she craves me just as much as I do her.

"We can add it to the list," I agree, though I am really not a fan of these shark attack films. "But we have to watch The Na'tra Temple after."

"You got yourself a deal, Daddy." Her smile is as bright as our suns.

We float for a while longer. On the beach people shout as they splash and play, but we are in our own bubble out on this part of the water. My hands flex and sneak under the bottom seams of her swimsuit. Odette sighs and it settles into my bones. I make her relaxed and at ease. My goals in life have shifted to centre her more. There are still plenty of things I do for my own enjoyment, but she is my everything.

The Axilarian suns begin their descent toward the horizon. We should head to our cottage soon, but neither of us seems interested in parting or leaving the water. A large wave washes into us and our bodies rock together harder, the steady tease stoking our needs higher and higher.

"We should go have a shower," Odette says, the look on her face telling me she wants more than to rinse off. "I'm getting hungry."

I'm already swimming us to shore, my tail propelling us most of the way. Once we're on the beach again, I keep behind my mate until I can wrap a towel around my waist. I'm aroused, but not crazy. Nobody here needs to see how much so.

We scramble to collect our things. It feels obvious what we're running back to our rental to do, but there isn't a being that pays us any mind. Odette practically skips up the stairs and peels off her wet suit. She steps into the rain station next to our front door and my mind goes blank.

Sweet Sur'lax.

I watched her wash away sand particles yesterday, and the day before that, and over a hundred times now. Still, I'm captivated by her beauty. The lush curves and rolls of her body, all the softness that cushions her form, it sings to me. My hands ache to squeeze her body, to be the water droplets that cling to her skin.

"Are you gonna join me or not, Daddy?"

I don't even bother undressing. She calls to me and I am there. Her touch is all I crave and when her hands tease my gills the shiver that rushes through my fins is electric. She giggles when I lift her up and press her back into the smooth stone walls of our alcove. Here, no one can see us.

But they can hear Odette sing for me.

My mouth descends on hers. She kisses me with a hunger that I have dreams about, ones where I wake up with a smile and hard cocks that I can tease my mate with in the early hours of the morning. Her body rocks against my torso like it did in the sea, a slow roll fueling the fire inside us both.

I shift my grip on her ass and begin shoving at my trunks. There is no part of me that is willing to wait. My need to sink into my mate is everything.

But these fucking pants won't come off.

One of Odette's hands slips from my side to between our bodies. She grunts a little at the awkward stretch, but then she's got a hold of my pants. She presses the button to release the tethers and they slip off my body like oil.

"Space pants," she giggles.

"What would I do without you, pup?"

"Die from lack of blood flow to your brain," she suggests with a smirk, but when I slide her body lower down my torso her words turn to a gasp.

The heads of my cocks tease her pussy lips, frills smearing precum to mix with her own juices. I inhale sharply when one head snags at her opening and I'm surrounded by the scent of her arousal. It clings to her skin, and to me where she has rubbed her arousal down my chest. It's better than any sweet rillin, better than any mating fluids.

Pure Odette on my skin.

"Fuck me, Daddy, I can't wait," she whimpers.

"What do good pups say?" I tease. I know we are both in a state of near insanity with our horniness. Otherwise, why would we be about to fornicate outside? But even as I line my lower cock up, the top one teases her clit.

There is a glimmer of sass in her eyes, she's ready to be a brat, but it softens into something else as she looks at me. The rain station cascades cool freshwater down our bodies and the suns still shine, but their sensation is nothing compared to the love I feel from Odette. Her fingers smooth over my chest and rest over my hearts.

"Love you, Ma'xon."

My knees shake. She has told me this so many times, showed me everyday, so I know it's true. Yet I am still left dumbfounded and love-drunk when she reminds me. I lift her high enough to press another thorough kiss to her lips. Odette opens up for me and teases my sharp teeth, hungry for me and I want to savour the taste of her like it's our first kiss.

She squeezes me with her thighs as she breaks the kiss. Her lips are spit slick and swollen when she commands me, "Now fuck me, *please*, Daddy."

"Anything for you, pup," I promise.

My cocks spurt more precum when I slide her down my front again. Her fingers wrap around my biceps as I set her over the bottom one. My fins tingle with anticipation, my tail flicks with agitation. My body is screaming at me to mate, to fuck this perfect cunt into oblivion.

But I can't stop looking at how big my top dick looks pressed into the roll of her belly, how the light purple frills on it almost blend with her stretch marks. Like we were always meant to find each other.

She is my everything.

"Look at me," I beg. "I need to see you when I stretch your pretty pussy open."

"Oh, fuck yes."

With her eyes on me, I slowly press our bodies together. Every little detail of her fills my vision as her wet heat surrounds my cock. Her lips part, her chest heaves as she inhales, and her eyes stay trained on me. The frills pulse and a shiver courses through me as I fill her completely.

Her moans echo around our rain station as I begin to move her up and down my cock like a pleasure toy, like she is mine for the taking. Her soft body jiggles, but her hard nails dig into my skin. Pinpoints of pain that urge me to fuck her harder, faster. My top cock smears fluid across her skin, lilac trails painting a masterpiece of my carnal love for her.

Odette doesn't take her eyes off me.

"Yes, Daddy, just like that. Right there, right there—" Her words cut off in a wail and her arousal sprays across my hips as her pussy clamps down around my cock.

"That's it pup," I groan in my efforts to keep moving.

I don't want this to end yet. Even though we have decades still to spend with each other, I can never settle for just one. Odette may not keep score, but the running tally in my head is always countin three to one. Some days it's higher, some days it's lower, but always, I want to watch the bliss take hold of my mate until she is well and truly fucked.

Without warning, I shift my grip. She miraculously takes my cock deeper as I rearrange us enough that my thumb squeezes between us. When I begin to swirl my finger around her clit in the motion she likes best, her eyes flutter close. Her pussy grips me harder, the stimulation beginning to overwhelm her.

"Just one more, Odette. Can you do that for Daddy?" I ask, panting as the strain on my muscles grows.

She nods and that's all I need. My hips return to the fast paced strokes that quickly brought on her first orgasm, but this time my thumb plays an uncoordinated melody on her clit as she screams for me. I don't know how long I last, it's not something I have ever cared about, but my need to spill comes on like a tidal wave. My focus has solely been on watching my mate fall apart that I forgot to register my own body. My tail suddenly locks up and my hips refuse to pull themselves away from my mate. I move my thumb against Odette's clit with more precision and just as she falls apart, so do I. My body shakes, tail flailing behind us as we are both swallowed by our climax.

My chest heaves with exertion. Odette's hands shake as she slides them through the mess I spilled across her torso. She brings a finger up to her mouth and licks it clean with a sigh.

"Love you, Daddy."

"Until we are one with the seas above, pup."

Her head falls to the side with a smile. Loose strands of hair cling to her neck, but I can see our mating bite. It's faded a little bit more with time, but it will never really go away. The little divot in her skin that I see her touching when she is reading one of her smutty earth books make my hearts sing.

I know our romance will have the happily ever after we deserve.

Thank you for reading!

If you liked this book, please remember to leave a review on your preferred sites to help other readers find my work.

None of this would have been possible without the amazing help from the generous and supportive people in my life. Thank you for never giving up on me.

Special shout out to-

- To Lyonne and Jen for listening to complain about Shark Daddy.

- To my beta team, I'm so sorry for all the typos, but your encouragement and kindness got me through it.

- To Sophie, Bonesy, and Laura for bringing my characters to life and making them so hot. Your talent leaves me in awe daily.

- To Kai for editing this crazy mess and not judging my wrong quotations.

- To Joy for not questioning me after reading my Kickstarter and letting pack all those boxes in your house.

Ash Raven is an indie author who specialises in spicy monster and alien romances that focus on plus-size and LGBTQ+ leads who get the love of a lifetime. They strive to write stories that are inclusive and real, with a touch of magic and a boat load of spice. When they are not writing, they are cuddling with their two orange cats and drinking oat mochas through a straw. Born and raised in Indiana, they have been living their own insta-love romance in London, UK since 2015.

Want to know more? You can find Ash on most social media as @authorashraven or subscribe to their newsletter for exclusive updates, art prints, and cat pictures.